A BODY IN THE LANE

Elizabeth Long

First published by Busybird Publishing 2023

ISBN
Paperback: 978-1-922954-36-7
Ebook: 978-1-922954-37-4

Cover design: Kev Howlett @ Busybird Publishing
Layout and typesetting: Maggie Turner @ Busybird Publishing

Busybird Publishing
2/118 Para Road
Montmorency, Victoria
Australia 3094
www.busybird.com.au

A Note on the Story

This novel is a spin off from *The Taroona Incident*. Although *A Body in the Lane* is unlike *The Taroona Incident* in storyline, some characters from the first novel are reintroduced. If you, the reader, have not read my first novel, and for the purposes of clarity and context, I would like to familiarise you with those characters.

Mark Amos is the stepson of Rebecca Amos (formerly Parke). She is now married to Andrew Amos father of Mark. Rebecca was previously married to Gary Smyth.

Imogen and Hughe Smyth are the parents of Gary and Eric Smyth.

Zac Harris, a long-time friend of Mark Amos, encouraged Mark to join the police force.

Lillian Parke is Rebecca's mother.

Hector is Lillian's cousin and Rebecca's second cousin.

1. Melbourne

1998

The laneway, located off Exhibition Street Melbourne, was dark and foreboding, resembling a rarely visited, deep, underground cave. The surrounding structure was wet with water running down the bluestone walls into a scant drain.

It was two am and cold. A soft drizzle was falling. Drops of rain collected on the shoulders of the detective's heavy coats, so lightly they didn't feel the increasing dampness slowly spreading through the fabric.

Homicide Detectives Mark Amos and Zac Harris were standing by a body lying in a dark corner beside a large, dirty, green skip. It lay there unnoticed by the foot traffic passing the narrow lane that never received the sun. The police presence was attracting a few onlookers who were sternly requested to move on.

'I've never seen anything like this,' said Mark.

'Me either,' said Zac.

The only entry into the laneway was now securely cordoned off by tape strung across the opening and flapping in the breeze. Two police officers and a sergeant stood close together on the footpath, occasionally remarking to each other or presenting a formidable, unspoken bearing to the general public.

Few people were in the city at this time of the morning, except for the many homeless persons sleeping under a variety of blankets beside the surrounding buildings, trying to keep warm and dry.

The rear door of a restaurant opened onto the end of the lane. A few rubbish bins had been placed along the back wall. A lone staff member, working the last shift, had discovered the body when emptying food leftovers. With a shaking hand he'd called triple zero.

Detectives lifted one end of a plastic sheet the uniforms used to cover the body, switched on their flashlights and were crouched over the motionless mound of a human being that was naked and lying on its side in the foetal position. The face of the corpse was twisted in torment, the hands splayed. They slowly moved the beams of their torches, searching for anything that would give them an inkling of what had happened.

Only one side of the face could be seen but there wasn't much left of it. There were bruises over the body, cigarette burns and slashes from what looked like knife cuts to the skin.

Sergeant Murphy came down and stood beside them. He was a man of twenty years experience in the police force. He handed them a folder containing written notes.

'Have you seen anything like this before?' asked Mark.

'Only once,' he said. 'Most of the dead I've seen are a result of gunshots or knife wounds. This person has been through a lot.'

'Forensics?' asked Mark.

'On their way.'

'Thanks, Sergeant.'

Newly appointed forensic officer, Peter Garcia, lifted the police tape and walked down the lane with a short, unhurried gait. A gust of wind blew both sides of his unbuttoned raincoat wide open, revealing a rotund figure. With hands clutching equipment, he made an attempt to keep his ample mop of hair in place while nodding to the sergeant who was on his way back to the street.

On reaching the crime scene, Garcia greeted the detectives. 'Hi, Peter Garcia, forensic pathologist. I'm the new guy. Not new at this sort of work, of course,' he said, with a modicum of humour and slightly out of breath.

'Detective Mark Amos and Detective Zac Harris,' said Mark. They shook hands.

'Well, what do we have here?' asked Peter.

'We were called out, arrived here about two this morning. A staff member from the restaurant found the body while emptying the rubbish bins,' said Mark.

'Quite a jolt, I expect,' said Peter.

'Yes. We haven't questioned anyone yet. The sergeant has. We wanted the body looked at as soon as possible because it's in the rain. Evidence could be running down the drain here.'

'Yes, right, let's have a look then, shall we?' Peter pulled on his surgical gloves, bent down and shone his torch, firstly over the face, down the exposed arm, over the chest, then the folded leg. He opened his case, retrieved a thermometer, took a rectal temperature, then set his compact weather station on the ground, recorded the ambient temperature and wrote down both results.

'Time of death?' asked Zac.

'Well, rigor hasn't set in just yet, so at a guess, and I say a guess, maybe between ten pm and midnight. I'll know more after the post mortem.'

Peter took a swab of the blood that was being washed away on the ground, just in case it revealed something. Then he knelt on the wet concrete, closer to the body, and lifted a part of the soft flesh to take another swab of blood that remained under the man's right side. Both swabs were secured into their separate, cylindrical containers. He wrote something on both and sealed them into a plastic bag then proceeded to take photos of the dead man at different angles. When finished he put his instruments away, shut his case, stood up and looked around the area.

'Not much blood around, considering his injuries. I would have expected it to be everywhere. Still, it has been raining. However, I think he was killed elsewhere. He doesn't have any clothes on either, so I assume he wasn't carrying any ID?' Peter didn't wait for a reply. 'Pretty fit man I would say, good muscle tone. That will disappear when rigor sets in, of course.'

'There's nothing in the notes to indicate any ID was found. I'll ask the sergeant in a minute, when the body has been taken away,' said Mark.

'We'll do a DNA test anyway. Right, well, let's get the police down here to remove the body. I'll stick around for that.'

'When do you think you could give us an idea of what has happened to him?' asked Zac.

'I would think we can start examining him first thing tomorrow. We have a few cases waiting for us to look at, but this one will take priority. We could give you a preliminary report late in the pm perhaps.'

'Right, thank you, Peter.'

They shook hands again.

The body of the dead man was put onto a stretcher, covered, and taken away to the morgue with Peter Garcia walking slowly behind.

Mark and Zac surveyed the ground where the body had been. They inspected the drain, the walls and the rubbish bins, inside and out. Nothing. Neither could they find a weapon.

Sergeant Murphy handed the detectives some more notes of his interview with the staff member of the restaurant and gave the them a verbal account of what had transpired.

'He was the only one left to clean up, usual procedure apparently. There wasn't a lot left to do. He was washing up the last of the pots and pans. Most of the restaurant was in darkness, apart from the kitchen. The building was locked up except the back door here. He leaves by that door and locks it from the outside then walks down Exhibition Street to his car. Apparently, none of the other kitchen staff empty these bins – that's his job. I've asked him about the patrons here today but he didn't see anyone else in the lane and never has. Tonight was an exception. He had nothing more to say. He was pretty freaked out. Frankly, I don't think he has anything to do with this, he just works here.'

'Was that the only time he came out here to the bins?' asked Mark.

'No. There are bins in the kitchen and when they're filled up he brings them out to empty them. Depending on the number of people it could be up to two or three times while the place is in full swing. He came out here about eight-ish but didn't notice anything. The last one was around one am. The smaller bins were full so he walked to the skip. That's when he noticed the body.'

'He didn't hear or see anything else?' asked Zac.

'Nothing. It's a pretty noisy, busy place inside, as you can imagine.'

Mark commenced reading the notes of the interview with the male staff member. 'Jacky Zhao?'

'Yep,' said Sergeant Murphy. 'He's Chinese. He's sitting in the kitchen waiting to be questioned.'

'Okay, thanks. We'll question him now. We'd like to keep the area closed off too please. We need to inspect it in daylight.'

'Sure. There's a change of shift. Two officers will sit in the van and keep an eye out. Do you want back up?'

'No, it's fine. We'll call if we do. Thanks, Sergeant,' said Zac. As the sergeant walked away, Zac turned to Mark. 'Do you think we'll get some sleep soon?'

'Clearly not,' said Mark who was writing notes of his own.

'Look, I'll leave the questioning of this Zhao guy to you. I'll go back to the office and start typing up a report about this. Meet you back there, okay?'

Mark looked up at Zac, surprised. 'Sure, sure, okay.' It was rare for Zac to opt out of the questioning stage of a case. He watched Zac walk away and briefly speak to the uniforms on the street before getting into his car.

Mark then entered the restaurant. It was dark except for the long kitchen. Bright lights shone down with a hot intensity. Various woks, utensils and plates sat on shining, stainless steel surfaces. Some had been cleaned but leftover morsels of food still remained on a few others.

Jacky Zhao was seated on a stool at the bench, his head in his hands, facing the darkness.

'Hello, Jacky, I'm Detective Mark Amos. I'm here to ask about what you saw earlier.'

Jacky looked around and swiftly slid off the stool. He wore a brown t-shirt along with loose, white pants. Both were oversized, making his slight frame look even leaner. Dried and wet stains were smeared over both garments as if someone had painted them on with a wide paintbrush. His fear was palpable.

'Please sit. You like some tea?'

'No, but thanks,' said Mark. 'Can you tell us what you saw?'

'I see man lying in lane. I have closer look and see what I can do. I know he is dead. I ring police on oh-oh-oh straight away. I no sleep now, I can still see in my head.'

'That must have been a shock,' said Mark.

'Yes, very, very shock. Who is he? What he doing in lane?'

'We don't know yet. Did you see anything else?'

Jacky sat for a moment, head tilted, thinking. 'Yes, yes,' he said, rather excitedly. 'Now I remember. When I empty out first bin early in night, a big man.' Jacky stood up. 'He much bigger than me.' He demonstrated with his arms and hands. 'He much bigger this way and this way. He walking this way.' Jacky spread his arms away from his body and above his head.

'What was he wearing?' asked Mark.

'I only see back of him; it was dark. I think he had a … what you call, shiny, no leather, yes, leather coat. It was long.'

'Anything else? Hair colour?'

'I think black, like me.'

'Can you think of anything else, Jacky?' asked Mark.

'I think I see big rings on hand. He was doing this as he walk away.' Jacky swung his arms back and forth, mimicking a strong walking manner. 'I see shine from light on street.'

'On this hand?' asked Mark, pointing to the left.

'Yes,' he confirmed.

Mark stood up. 'Thank you, Jacky, you have helped a lot. Will you come to work tomorrow?' asked Mark.

'No, I ring uncle and stay home. I am not sleeping tonight, I think. He will know. He is good boss.'

'He owns the restaurant?'

'Yes, he owns.'

'How long have you been working here?'

Jacky looked down at his hand, studying his fingers. 'I here nearly three years.'

'Okay, well, thank you. You ring us if you think of anything else or need help.' Mark handed him his card.

'Thank you, yes, yes this is good.' Jacky smiled, took the card and bowed to Mark.

'Are you feeling all right to drive home? Do you live by yourself?'

'Yes, thank you, I okay. I finish here then go home, is not far. I have special cup of tea. I live by myself but I okay.' He bowed.

Mark decided to wait until Jacky finished cleaning up then escorted him up the lane, under the tape and onto the footpath where they shook hands. He was watched intently as he got into his car and drove away.

'Any more clues? What do you think of him?' asked Sergeant Murphy. He was still standing on the footpath with the other officers, changing from one foot to another and blowing on his hands to keep them warm.

'First impression? I agree with you, I don't think he's a killer. For a start, he doesn't look like he would have the strength to inflict a body with those deep wounds. Also, he wouldn't have the time and what's his motive? I believe him. He looks shocked; he didn't know the guy. Nah, he didn't do it.' Mark looked at his watch. Time was getting on; it was now four fifty-five am. He briefly spoke with the uniforms to confirm police and police tapes were in place to protect the laneway, then he drove to the station. Zac was still at his desk.

'I thought you'd be a certainty to join me in questioning Jacky Zhao.'

'Yeah, sorry, mate, but I don't feel up to that intense stuff right now.'

'What's wrong, Zac?' asked Mark.

'Nothing, nothing serious, just feeling tired. I'm beginning to think working these hours is not in line with my body clock. Maybe I'm getting old.'

Mark gave him a nudge. 'You poor old soldier. Living alone is not good for you, you need to be with someone.'

'Yeah, yeah, yeah, so you keep telling me. Anyway, fill me in, how did it go?'

Mark relayed specifics of his talk with Jacky Zhao.

'It's six am, Zac. I'm knocking off, what about you?' Mark asked.

'Yep, me too.'

With the closing of computers and tidying up of their desks, the two walked together to the car park and said their goodnights.

Zac and Mark had known each other a long time. They were more than colleagues; they were good mates. Zac convinced Mark to join the police force and he never regretted it. Both worked diligently through the ranks and rose to become detectives two years ago. They were rarely able to pair up during the day but usually requested each other for the night shift. It wasn't always achievable, but tonight was one of those nights and they were glad of it. Each had their own strengths; they worked well together and were recognised for their successes by others in the branch.

Many crimes had been solved by these two, but some were still open for further investigation. Arson and death at a warehouse, assisting the drug squad with a raid of a bikies gang hangout, which yielded nothing, but they were not giving up. A young woman's body found floating in the Yarra and a break-in at a house in Carlton, which was ruthless in its invasion and assault, leaving one member of the household still recovering in hospital.

There was a nagging in Mark's mind about Zac's actions of late. It was his inattentiveness to some files and a lack of his former enthusiasm. He was sometimes late for work and often took a back seat when questioning suspects. That alone was out of character. Mark couldn't figure out what was behind it. Then he shrugged it off and chastised himself for doubting his partner. *He's tired, needs a break,* he thought.

Mark was going home to his beautiful Julie. It had taken a while for him to settle down. There had been a series of women in his life. He was of medium height. An attractive man with a captivating grin, luxurious brown hair and dark brown eyes. Clothes he wore were off the rack. He was lucky because they always fitted perfectly and sat well on his toned physique. Very little coaxing was needed to find someone to partner with, however, none were serious enough for him to make a commitment.

Julie was different. She was stunning to look at, statuesque with auburn hair and hazel eyes. But more than that, she was clever, articulate and exercised compassion for those less fortunate. She worked for a charity organisation as an analyst and enjoyed it.

'I would like to be more hands on though,' she often said.

She was a realist and knew Mark would need to be on the job at odd hours; it didn't bother her as long as he came home unhurt. Both were in their thirties; Julie was three years younger than Mark. There had been talk about having children but they still couldn't decide. At least this indecision was mutual, no arguments on that front. They argued about other things, visiting her parents for one. He just couldn't relate to them. He tried with all-out efforts over five years. It was a mystery to him, and to Julie. But she insisted he keep trying.

'Of course, they like you. You're being paranoid.'

'No, I'm not,' replied Mark, defensively. 'A gathering with them is like a visit to the museum – lots to look at, along with restrained comments.'

'Now that's a stupid analogy.'

'I think it's because we have absolutely nothing in common except you,' said Mark. 'I don't play golf, I haven't read the latest book, I don't have time to go to the theatre. They've retired and have time to indulge themselves in anything that pleases them. All I can talk about is my work and the majority of that is mostly confidential. You know that.'

'Alright, alright,' Julie said in surrender.

Julie's mother was a retired librarian and her father had worked in insurance. Both of them seemed unexcited by life in general. Mark couldn't break through or ignite a spark in them. He deeply loved his wife and that mattered most to him.

He tiptoed into the house, undressed and got in to bed beside his still sleeping wife. She felt warm and he passed his hand gently over her curves. His erection was immediate, he wanted to make love with her but accepted this was not a good time; she didn't like being woken. So he turned over to his other side where sleep gradually supressed his desire.

Zac Harris didn't have that certain look to charm women so easily. He was a bit shorter than Mark with black hair, a pale face and rather ample nose. But countering these incumbrances was his perfect, white, generous smile. As a result, some women found him very attractive. But he wasn't looking; no particular females' attention turned him on. There were moments of loneliness, but his job was his life and meant far more to him. If someone came along, fine, but if not, well, he wasn't going to dwell too much.

Zac never went straight home at the end of a shift. If it was in the early hours of the morning, he'd buy a coffee from one of the few street vendors open at that hour. They knew him well. He'd stand and take a few sips from the cup, think about the shift he'd just finished. Did he achieve anything positive? Probably not.

The rain had stopped momentarily and the sun was just coming up. Looks like it's going to be fine and sunny today, he thought. Exhaustion came over him suddenly. 'God, I'm tired of this,' he murmured to himself, as he slowly walked to his car.

2. Melbourne

Hughe Smyth was a tall, distinguished-looking man with abundant, grey, well-groomed hair. He wore tailor-made suits, which further enhanced his elegant and refined image. A strong jaw completed his unlined face except for a few, just visible on his forehead. And he spoke with a deep, quiet voice when giving advice. Sentences were measured, solicitous. He completed a session with a well-practised wide smile. Some found it artificial. The fees he charged were exorbitant too, but his clients didn't question it. He was deemed the best and they were prepared to pay for his expertise, talent and undeniable knowledge of the law.

His practice had expanded to Melbourne, where he spent three days and the other two in Hobart. He had assistants at both: a young man in Hobart who was a university graduate and in Melbourne an older woman with extensive experience as a legal secretary.

In his Melbourne rooms, just beyond the reception area, was an office where Hughe could offer privacy behind closed doors. It was basic in design with white walls. A framed photo of his wife and a neat pile of files sat on a large mahogany desk. Facing his desk were two matching, leather-studded chairs, providing a sense of good taste and comfortable seating for his clients. In a corner, by the large, floor to ceiling window, was a cabriole-leg lamp table, which supported a slender, glass vase overflowing with fresh flowers, changed every day at his request. One wall was covered floor to ceiling by bookcases lined with volumes related to law, in neat rows and exact numerical order.

Sometimes Hughe would stand at the window staring at the people below, feeling secure, safe and far removed from the ordinary man. Then he would resume his work with a feeling of complacency. But recently things had changed. Now his days were filled with persistent anxiety. To everyone else, though, he held up the façade of self-assurance.

There was a client with Hughe and his secretary could hear raised voices.

'Look, I can't do anything now, I'll attend to it tomorrow, first thing, I promise. I'm expecting my son any minute. You have to leave. Now!' said Hughe, shouting and pleading.

'Make sure you do, right? Just do it,' said the man in a loud, threatening voice.

'I will, I will,' said Hughe, agitated.

Alarmed, the secretary had picked up the phone and hit zero, then zero again. Suddenly the client stomped out, his face red with anger. Ignoring the secretary, he opened the door forcibly and exited down the stairs. Hughe came out of his office.

'Are you okay, Mr Smyth?' She always addressed her boss formally.

'Yes, yes, I'm fine, thank you. You can't please everyone, can you?' he said, trying to brush it off, act as if this meeting was a normal interaction.

'Can I do anything, sir?'

'No, thank you, Margaret,' Hughe said, gaining his composure. 'My son, Gary, will be here shortly. Just let him in please.'

'Of course, Mr Smyth.'

Hughe and his son were going to have a long lunch together. He hadn't seen or heard much from Gary for a year and was looking forward to catching up at last.

Hughe never admitted to a having a favourite son. Gary was the oldest. He was gregarious, daring and radiated positivity accompanied by a generous grin. The younger son, Eric, was the opposite. He was studious, quiet, taciturn. *Eric is more like me,* he often thought.

Gary climbed the stairs to see his father. He knew he had been tardy in communicating with his family. But then, he had been in far outback places for months on end. Connecting had sometimes been challenging. He had a satellite phone but kept that for emergencies. He contacted his mother more frequently than his father – he was closer to her.

A large, brawny man bumped into him as he ascended the stairs. He stared right at Gary for what seemed liked a few seconds then restarted down without apology.

Rude prick, thought Gary. He walked into the reception area of his father's practice.

'Hello,' he said to the secretary. 'Margaret, isn't it?'

'Yes, you are Gary?'

'I am,' he said, shaking her hand.

'Please go straight in. Your father is expecting you.'

He thanked Margaret and entered his father's office. He found him head down, reading something. He looked up; his face was grave, frown lines now more prominent.

'Seeing me is not that bad, is it?'

'Oh, sorry, son, I was thinking about a case. So good to see you.' Hughe came around to the front of his desk and embraced his son. 'It's been far too long.'

'My fault, Dad, sorry. The outback is not conducive for reliable communication and no sooner have I finished one guided tour, I'm off again. Time flies – before I know it another year has passed.'

'It's fine, son. As long as you are well and happy. Shall we go out for a drink and something to eat? I've cleared my appointments for the day. Margaret can lock up when she's finished.'

'Yep, as long as you're paying,' Gary said, with one of his familiar cheeky grins.

Father and son came out together to the reception area. Hughe closed the door to the inner office then checked it, making sure it was securely locked.

'I won't be back today, Margaret. Just lock up when you're finished. See you tomorrow.'

'Of course, Mr Smyth. Have a lovely time together. See you tomorrow.'

'She's very formal,' Gary said as they went down the stairs.

'That's just her way. I'm happy for her to call me by my Christian name but she won't have it. She's old school. I couldn't do without her.'

'Where are we going?'

'How about Chinatown? There are some good restaurants there.'

'Sounds perfect,' said Gary.

The Chinese restaurant father and son were experiencing was an expensive, lavish place. Eating areas were divided by floor to ceiling dividers, some in simple design, others more complex. Each narrow column was spaced exactly to enable a patron to see others seated at tables but not able to hear any dialogue. Every divider was painted red. And the many lampshades hanging from the ceiling had a golden hue. Red chairs were soft and comfortable; waiters spoke in hushed tones and walked from a table promptly to dispense an order to the chefs.

An hour had passed. Gary and Hughe had shared a banquet for two. Both felt satisfied at the end of their lunch and were relaxing with a beer.

'God, so much food. I don't think I could eat another thing for twenty-four hours,' said Gary.

'I know, filling, isn't it? You look tanned and well, Gary,' said Hughe, a little envious of his son's lifestyle.

'A bonus of the job, I suppose. I work at it though, Dad. It's a considerable task taking people out into the never-never where anything could happen. As you know, I'm heavily insured and take precautions. So far, so good. I'm trained in first aid, always take lots of water with us and my satellite phone. I've purchased another very trusty ex-Army Land Rover and my maximum is six people so it's pretty safe. I do go to these places by myself too, just to check them out, so to speak. Katherine and surrounds are favourites. Not sure if I told you, but I have a mate with me sometimes and he stays behind and sets up a campfire and dinner at night. Couldn't do without him on those nights. I'm pretty tired at the finish of those long walks. During the day I head off with the guests and we do a bit of trekking around. We like to keep outside the usual tourist areas. Gives them a feeling of being the only ones.'

'Have you improved the sleeping arrangements?' asked Hughe, knowing Gary's habit of having everyone sleep under the stars in any weather.

'Yes, I have quite a large tent now. It's all hands-on deck in helping erect it, part of the fun and experience. Everyone sleeps in there with their own sleeping bag. They are spaced out so they don't encroach on each other. We can't do anything about the snorers though and the odd bit of farting.' They both laughed.

'Do you miss teaching?' asked his father.

'Nope, not for a second. I love the outdoor life. One of my best decisions was to move to Alice. How are Mum and Eric?'

'Well, Mum is happy. She has plenty of friends, the house is her pride and joy and she is totally enamoured with the new Mercedes I just bought her. She has expensive tastes, your mother. She misses you, of course. Eric is well. His two girls are growing up. He and Cynthia are happy too, thankfully. She thinks Eric prefers playing in the orchestra far more than being with her. She's joking, of course. What about you? Have you met someone yet? You're getting older, you know,' said Hughe.

'No, sadly. I think I've left it too late really. I've yet to meet someone who loves continually being outdoors like me.'

'Are you okay for money?' asked Hughe.

'Oh, sure. I guess I can always do with a bit extra but I'm not starving. I have somewhere nice to live in Alice Springs and a basic little place in Katherine where I stay during the tourist season. I have a good life, I'm not complaining. You and Mum should come and stay sometime.'

'Yes, we should. Here, take this.' Hughe handed him an envelope under the table.

'No, Dad, I'm fine.'

'Please take it. There's a couple of grand in there.'

'You sure? Wow, thanks, Dad,' said Gary, taking the envelope and putting it straight into his pocket. Though feeling slightly uncomfortable by the offer, he needed a bit of financial help just now. Besides, his father enjoyed helping his sons and Gary was not about to spoil the moment.

'Talking about getting on, when are you retiring?'

'I plan to do that in the next few months. I'm not taking on any more clients here in Melbourne. I'll finish off the cases for my existing clients then do the same in Hobart. I want to relax and enjoy what's left of my life.'

'So you should, you've been doing this for a long time.' Gary started preparing to leave. 'I'd better go, Dad. I have an early flight back. I need to get some sleep.' He picked up his backpack and slung it over his shoulder.

'Of course. Contact me when you get back, just so I know you have arrived safely,' said Hughe.

'Will do. See you, Dad. Hopefully it won't be a year this time and thanks for the money.'

'Let me know if you need anything. I'm always able to help, son.'

They hugged each other and Hughe watched his son leave. He would miss him, as always.

On the following day and after finishing off a case and giving Margaret instructions, Hughe caught a late flight back to Hobart.

3. Melbourne

Mark and Zac were watching from the viewing room as the pathologist and his technician worked on the body of the man found in the laneway. They had prepared a report for the coroner noting it was a reportable death. There were still no clues concerning a next of kin. At this stage, they had little to work with.

Mark was glad they weren't in the same white, sterile room as the body. He had been, just once before, and felt ill. Embarrassingly for him, he vomited outside. The look of a dead human form being cut open, along with the strong, pervading odour of chemicals turned his stomach. Those around him sympathised. They, at some time, had also experienced the same revulsion. Their first sight of the slicing open of a chest, the strong stench of formaldehyde and other substances had also sent them outside, bent over, spraying the grass with the contents of their last meal. Most would calm down then staunchly walk back inside.

'This guy suffered a great deal,' said Peter Garcia. He looked up at them through the glass while speaking through an intercom.

'Yeah, we thought it looked pretty bad,' said Zac.

'Can you tell us something of what you have found please, Peter?' asked Mark.

'Yes, well, the left side of his face has been severely damaged, as you know. I suggest it was perhaps a baseball bat, a cricket bat, a golf club or other similar implement wielded to the face with force several times, I would think. Haven't found any splinters or other material at this stage though.

'There is a hairline fracture to the skull. Teeth on that side of his face are broken. The other side of his face is intact. There are no fillings so we can't identify him that way. A few fingernails are missing and he has cigarette burns to many parts of his body as well as knife cuts to his chest and abdomen. His left arm is broken and bruised. I'm guessing this may have happened as he was trying to defend himself from the blows to his face, but that's a maybe at this early stage. We haven't done every test yet; some have gone off for chemical analysis. I would be amazed if he was a drug taker, so far there's nothing to suggest it. My first view of him in the laneway confirmed he was fit. There was also pooling of blood on the side of the body where he was laying. But I still don't think he had been there very long.

'It will take up to two to three weeks before toxicology reports are back, that is, when I send some tissue samples. I'll also get some DNA from his cheeks and hair. See if that helps us.'

'Okay, no earlier than that?' asked Mark.

'Afraid not, I'll do my best. I know you want to identify him.'

'Thanks, and yes, we do. We can't go any further until you give us something.'

They farewelled Peter and the corpse he was surveying, and headed back to their cars. Mark decided to do another inspection of the lane. Zac said he couldn't go with him – he had another report to attend to, so he drove back to the station.

The tape had been removed. Mark walked down the lane slowly, inspecting the walls and ground again as he traversed the slight slope towards the back where the rubbish bins stood. It was a bright, sunny day but the prevailing weather didn't penetrate the surrounding bluestone that still looked grey and damp. Laughter and noise filtered through the screen of the restaurant's back door. It was lunchtime and busy. The aroma of Asian food pervaded everywhere. Mark realised he was hungry. He had spent half an hour of concentrated inspection then walked back to the front of the restaurant and entered. It was louder inside; every table was occupied. The place was filled with talk. Whiffs of aromas and clatter came from the kitchen. He picked up a menu and spent a moment scanning the list. A young Asian woman came from somewhere to serve him. 'Good afternoon, can I help you?'

'Yes, thank you. Do you do take away?' asked Mark.

'Yes of course, what would you like?' she asked with a polite voice and a full smile.

'The black bean combination please.'

'Certainly, sir, please take a seat. It will be ready in about ten minutes.'

'Is Jacky in today?' Mark enquired.

'No, he is unwell today. Do you know him?'

'Only briefly. What about the owner?'

'No, he is not in today. Can I take a message?'

'No, that's fine, thank you.' Mark didn't want to identify himself as a detective just now. He would follow up when more of what had happened became clearer.

The woman gave him a perplexed look over her shoulder on her way to arrange his order. The detective in him couldn't resist surreptitiously searching the place with practised eyes, taking in every detail, storing it in his memory. He did it automatically, like changing gears in a car. In time he would relive it, speculate, focus on other aspects.

On arriving back at the station, Mark offered Zac a share of his black bean takeaway.

'No thanks, mate, no appetite today.'

'That's not like you. Are you okay?' Mark remarked, with a friendly push to Zac's arm.

'Yep, fine. Busy, though.'

Mark took the hint, peeled off his jacket and sat down to eat. He was starving.

4. Hobart

'You tossed and turned most of the night.' Imogen was rather annoyed at her husband for interrupting her sleep. She had forgotten to take her sleeping tablet. 'Are you uneasy about Gary?'

'Did I? Sorry. Lot on my mind, I suppose, and no, Gary is doing well. He's fine,' said Hughe.

'I'm glad you're nearing retirement. It's getting beyond you. You haven't been the same for a while. I know I've asked before but can't you tell me what's wrong?'

'There's nothing to tell you, Imogen. I have a lot of clients and cases to deal with. You're right, though, it is wearing me down. Just a few more weeks and I'll be finished with it. I have another lawyer friend who's happy to buy out my practice. Both here and Melbourne.'

'Who?' she asked.

'Johnathan Lewis.'

'Good choice. He's young and clever I'm told.'

'Who told you that?' he asked, surprised.

'You know how word gets around in Hobart, it's a gossipy place; everyone knows other people's business.'

'Yes, that's true,' he said.

A long silence arose between them. Suddenly, Hughe came up with an idea. 'Why don't we move interstate? What about Alice Springs, for example? We would be closer to Gary.'

Imogen was aghast. 'What? Why would we do that? Aren't you happy here? We would miss our friends, our house, our grandchildren, the beauty of this state. Why would we move? Gary can come back whenever he wants. He knows that. What's going on with you?'

'Nothing really, I'm a bit restless, I suppose. At least let's do some tripping around the country when I finish up. What do you think?' Hughe asked.

'Sure, if you want to. I could do some researching on places to stay and the best time to go there. I'll talk to a few of our friends, get some advice. You do remember we have a fundraiser here next weekend?'

'Yes, yes. I haven't forgotten. Getting it catered for as always?' he asked.

'Of course. We'll have about a hundred here.'

They walked out of the kitchen. Imogen went to her writing desk and Hughe to the bathroom.

Hughe was thinking while having a long shower. Unlike previous times, he wasn't looking forward to the evening. He had too much on his mind and didn't feel like socialising. Pretence of interest in any sort of banter was going to be taxing.

The Smyth's held fundraisers twice a year. One for The Red Cross and the other for The Smith Family. These nights were full of fun accompanied by excellent food as well as a parlour game, usually trivia. Guests were generous. Proceeds were deposited into a bank account and a cheque for the total amount given to the charities. Contributors were sent a copy of the receipt as confirmation of their munificence.

Imogen was in her element on these occasions. There was no end to her vainglorious tendencies. She always wore a new outfit at every fundraiser, along with her expensive jewellery. Every inserted jewel was genuine, every exquisite piece encased in gold. She bought her gowns in Melbourne and her jewellery was custom designed to her specific requirements. Hughe had a permanently booked hotel suite near his rooms that enabled him to service his Melbourne clients. Imogen would periodically fly in to stay with him. It was at these times she would further indulge herself and visit selected boutique shops at the top end of Collins Street.

When friends asked the designer of her stunning gowns, she would proudly display the label for them to admire. Many oohs and aahs ensued and Imogen would feel her heart flutter with excitement.

There were one or two women who viewed Imogen differently. They saw her as self-indulgent, attention-seeking and vain. But they were in the minority and neither spoke of it to each other. In spite of their disapproval, they attended anyway because it was exclusive and prestigious. Being there confirmed their high status in the social scene.

It was noticed the typically unflappable Hughe Smyth was not himself on the night of their latest gathering. He seemed edgy, restless.

'Are you well, Hughe?' asked one of his long-time friends.

'Yes, yes, of course, why do you ask?'

'Because I don't think you've heard one word I've said.'

'Oh! Sorry, Mike. Just thinking about a troubling case. What were you saying?

The entire discourse was like this for Hughe. Imogen had to constantly remind him of his tasks. She wondered if this was the beginning of dementia or perhaps, he'd suffered stroke without realising it. She would insist he visit the doctor.

In truth, Hughe was attempting to hide his unrelenting distress. Under no circumstances could he confide it to anyone.

5. Melbourne

Two days after the body in the lane was discovered

The detectives had been able to pair up again, this time during the day shift. First task for the day was a follow up with Jacky Zhao, just in case something was missed at the first interview. They were at the restaurant; a waitress came forward to greet them. On seeing their IDs, she took them through the kitchen out to the back of the restaurant. It was around four and several cooks were busy preparing food for the never-ending patrons who were conversing, drinking, eating or waiting for the next course.

The kitchen was suggestive of street sellers in an Asian market. Men moving from one hot plate to another, flames flaring and subsiding, spices being shaken into woks that were tossed to move food around for consistency of cooking, while constantly conversing with each other in their native language. The aroma of Asian food pervaded everywhere and, as usual, Mark was salivating.

'How can I help you?' the waitress asked.

'We just wanted to talk to Jacky for a moment. Is he about?'

'No, he didn't come in again today.'

'Is his uncle in?' asked Zac.

'No, sorry. He's interstate for business reasons.'

'Do you work here? Are you a relative?' asked Mark.

'No, I only work part time here and I'm not a relative. I'm studying at uni. Is anything wrong?' She was becoming uneasy.

'No, it's fine. We just wanted to ask Jacky a few more things. He was very helpful the last time we spoke,' said Mark.

'Is this about the dead body in the lane out the back?'

'Do you know something?' asked Zac.

'Only brief reports I read in the paper and talk here amongst the staff. It's been very unsettling.'

'Yes, I understand, it would. Okay, well, thank you. We'll come back another time. What is the owner's name?'

'Mr Li. Do you want me to give him your card so he can contact you when he comes back?'

'No, we'll contact him, thank you.'

The detectives decided to call around to Jacky's place to check on his wellbeing and ask if he remembered anything else.

The detectives parked at the rear of the shop where Jacky lived. They climbed up the rusted metal stairs and knocked on the door. It opened slightly. Mark warned of his approach. No one answered. He slowly pulled a gun from his holster and motioned for Zac to stay outside on the landing.

On entering Mark could see Jacky lived in two rooms. One was a combined kitchenette and eating area with a faded table and two chairs. There was also a green, threadbare lounge chair and a couch that had a pull-out bed. The blankets and sheet had been folded back on one side. There was an indentation on the mattress where someone had been sleeping. The room was scattered with the few possessions Jacky owned, some of it broken. A pungent smell of dampness pervaded the space.

For a moment Mark couldn't speak, his mind was racing, his heart pounding – he felt sick. He found Jacky slumped on the floor in the bathroom with a bullet hole in his forehead and a trickle of blood that had run down the bridge of his nose.

'Oh, Jesus,' said Mark out loud. 'Who would want to kill this guy? He's just a kid, for Christ's sake!' He felt Jacky's neck with his fingers, hoping to detect a pulse. There was nothing – Jacky was dead.

'Ask for a pathologist, police and an ambulance please, Zac,' he shouted. 'Jacky's dead. Shit. Shit.' Mark was visibly affected. Sweat appeared on his forehead, bewilderment and disbelief wrestled with logic. He looked around but didn't want to compromise the scene, so he retraced his steps back to the outside and stood with Zac.

'On their way,' said Zac. 'What's your thoughts?'

'I think this has something to do with the body in the lane but for the life of me I don't know what yet.'

'Right. He seemed a good kid,' said Zac coolly.

'Yeah. What kind of sick bastards would do this?'

'You know the drill, mate, try not to get emotional,' Zac reminded him.

'Yeah, yeah, I know. Bloody impossible not to at times like these.'

Mark noticed a lack of empathy from Zac yet again. It was indeterminate, but it was there. Perhaps it was time for Zac to take a break. He definitely needed a holiday in a warm place somewhere. He'd talk to him about it later.

The pathologist arrived first. 'We meet again,' said Peter, who was accompanied by an assistant. 'What do we have this time?'

'A young Chinese guy who works at the restaurant where we found the body in the lane,' said Mark.

'Hmm, interesting. Coincidence, do you think?'

'Don't know yet, but my gut says no, it's no coincidence,' said Mark.

Peter proceeded to cover his feet and hands and put on a gown, as did his assistant. He handed shoe coverings to the detectives. 'Well, let's have a look then.'

The three walked to the minuscule bathroom. There was no door to it and only one person at a time could fit into the room. The others stood by the doorframe as Peter did his investigation. First thing was to close Jacky's eyes, then he focused on the hole in his forehead. He took a swab, photos and looked at other parts of his body as well as the temperature comparisons.

Mark and Zac turned, looked around the main room. They were standing on a fading timber floor. There were a few utensils placed on a tea towel sitting on the bench of the small kitchen, along with a single electric hot plate with a wok on top. The overhead shelf displayed a couple of coffee mugs and two large glass containers. One filled with rice and the other half-filled with assorted biscuits. There were six bowls beside these and balancing on them were two pairs of chopsticks. The shelf was bowed in the centre. The items sitting on it had moved to the edge and looked as if they were about to fall off.

A bar fridge, located in the corner of the room, emitted a low hum. Mark opened the door to find a collection of cans of soft drink, aging dairy items and sagging, lifeless greens.

There was a white laminated bedside table. On it stood a shaded lamp that had fallen on its side, and a book was on the floor. Zac picked it up and vigorously shook the pages.

'It's a book about learning to speak English.'

'God, this is depressing,' said Mark. 'A kid putting in an effort, living simply, doing his best to fit in, learning English. What danger could he be to anyone? I don't for one minute think it's drugs, so what the hell can it be? Why was he murdered?'

'No, nothing seemed suspicious about him,' said Zac in agreement.

Peter awkwardly squeezed his frame out from the bathroom. His assistant entered and proceeded to dust for fingerprints. A sergeant came to the door asking for the detectives.

'Hello, Sergeant, what would you like to know?' asked Zac.

'Apart from us, that is the only other car parked here.' He pointed to a white Ford Laser. 'We checked the registration. It's in the name of a Jacky Zhao. Is that the guy in there?'

'It is,' confirmed Mark.

'Ok, we haven't touched it yet. Could you get the pathologist to come and dust it for fingerprints then we can search it when he's finished?' asked the sergeant.

'Will do. I think he's nearly finished here.'

Peter Garcia joined them at the front doorway. His assistant did more fingerprint dusting then went to dust the Ford.

'Any clue of time of death Peter?' asked Zac.

'Je ne sais quoi,' said Peter with a flourish.

'What?' asked Mark.

'Sorry, sorry, bad timing. I'm learning French. Ah, right, well I would say sometime late last night, say eleven pm or midnight maybe.'

'What did that mean, that French stuff? asked Mark.

'*I do not know what*. Can't help myself. I wanted to learn another language other than English and Spanish. I love French, very romantic. I've been practising speaking it. Sorry, not the place. Well, down to the car, shall we?' Peter left to join his assistant inspecting the car, leaving Mark rather bemused.

The police came in to look at the scene and talk to the detectives. When they were satisfied and had gathered all information, Jacky was lifted into an ambulance and taken to the morgue. His front door was closed, police tapes placed around it, along with another tape across the first tread of the steps.

Focus was now on the car. It hadn't been locked. The boot was checked along with the glove box and under the seats. Nothing was found. It would be taken back to police headquarters and searched more thoroughly. At this stage, nobody expected to find anything helpful.

Police and Zac went back to type up reports while Mark and another detective went straight to the restaurant. The waitress confirmed Mr Li, owner of the restaurant, had been away for the last few days and wouldn't return to the restaurant until tomorrow. She gave them his address and contact number.

At the appointed time, Mr Li was visited by Mark and two other uniforms. He lived in a single-fronted property in Church Street. The façade of the dwelling had been updated with a fresh coat of paint along with a new front door and an ornate brass knocker. By contrast, the interior of the house still held pungent odours of its past history. Mr Li verified he had just arrived back; his unpacked luggage was still standing in the hallway. There was a look of astonishment about him as he beckoned them to the kitchen.

'You like to sit?' he asked.

'No, thank you, Mr Li. Have you spoken to your staff at the restaurant?' asked Mark.

'No, no speak. Why?'

'I'm afraid we have some bad news.'

'Oh no, restaurant burn down,' said Mr Li, shaking his head in dismay.

'Why would you say that?'

A moment of silence then Mr Li said, 'Bad luck, man dead in lane.'

'Your restaurant has not burnt down. I'm sorry to inform you your nephew Jacky Zhao is dead.'

'How he dead?' Mr Li's eyes opened wider; he grimaced and looked shaken.

'It's still under investigation, Mr Li. He has been taken to the morgue. We would like to take you there to identify him.'

'Is bad luck?' he asked.

'No, Mr Li, it will be okay, we can take you,' Mark assured him.

They drove him to the morgue where he identified his nephew Jacky Zhao. He wiped tears from his eyes. On the way back to his house, Li was assured they would get to the bottom of what had happened. Li alighted from the car without a word. He kept combing his surroundings as he walked to his house, then he opened the door and slammed it shut with a thud.

Back at the station Mark brought Zac up to date. 'By the way, Julie and I are going to Dad and Rebecca's for dinner. Would you like to join us?'

'Thanks, but I'm going to have a bit of a rest tonight, I'm buggered.'

'No worries, another time then,' said Mark.

6. Melbourne

The main meal had finished and those at the table were talking in between placing cheese and biscuits into their mouths. Mark and his dad were having a friendly debate about the political climate of the day.

'Have you made any decision yet?' Rebecca knew this was a delicate subject so asked Julie in a gentle, whispered tone.

'Frankly, I think we like the way things are. We're both dedicated to our jobs and each other. Plus, I'd have to give up this stuff,' Julie said, taking a sip of her favourite red with a wry smile. 'You didn't have any. Why not, may I ask?'

'Long story. But in short, by the time I found Andrew, it was physically too late,' said Rebecca.

'Any regrets?'

'When I see Andrew and Mark together there is a bit of longing, but I'm a happy chappy, I like things the way they are. I love Andrew, and Mark and I get on marvellously now – there are compensations.'

'Mark admires you, you know,' said Julie.

'Well, I admire him. I've heard he is an outstanding detective and performed well to get there. Right, who's for Scrabble?' Rebecca asked.

'Nope, you beat us most of the time, Bec. Tonight, we are going to make it a fairer competition. We are playing Pictionary.' Andrew was emphatic. Everyone groaned.

'Bec can draw too, Dad, remember?'

'Yes, I know, but we can do simple images. You don't have to be an artist like smarty-pants here,' Andrew said, pointing to Rebecca with a broad smile on his face.

They cleared the table in preparation for the contest.

It was the middle of the game and Rebecca was trying to make out something Julie had drawn. It baffled her. Mark's mobile rang.

'I thought you were going to turn that off,' said Julie disapprovingly.

'I've got to take this, sorry, everyone.' Mark went outside to the deck while the others kept playing and talking.

'He just can't relax,' Julie said, shaking her head.

A short time later Mark re-entered.

'Are you okay, son?' Andrew asked.

'Yeah, yeah, I'm okay.'

'Can you tell us what's going on?' asked Rebecca.

'Zac didn't sign in his firearm today. Not only that, no one can get hold of him. They've called him and gone around to his house. It's in darkness. His car is not there either. It's strange; he seemed okay today. I invited him around for tonight too. He said he was tired and wanted to get an early night. Not like him to refuse a night with you guys.' Mark was disturbed by the news. This was out of character for Zac.

Everyone at the table was quiet now, pondering on where he might have gone.

'It's funny, you know. At times I thought I was imagining it but … he hasn't been quite the same in the last few months,' said Mark.

'In what way?' Julie asked.

'Not quite as sharp. Sometimes his mind would be distracted by something else. It's a subtle change that no one else seems to have picked up, but we've known and worked closely together for a long time. I can sense it. Can't put my finger on it though, like other things I'm working on at the moment.' He gave a deep sigh and tried to get back into the game, but he couldn't stop thinking about Zac. Something was amiss.

In the end everyone stopped playing and spent time supporting Mark.

'I'm sorry to spoil the night,' Mark said apologetically while giving his step-mother a brief hug.

'No need,' said Rebecca.

Mark knew this interruption would frustrate his wife. There had been too many lately. Julie was a patient, caring person but did have her limits.

'Darling, so sorry,' Mark said when he and Julie were in the car.

'Of course. I know I get pissed off at times but I do get it. I suppose you want to check out his house?'

'Yep.'

'Okay. I want to come with you.'

'You sure?'

'Yes,' said Julie.

Zac lived in the front unit of a single row of six located in South Yarra. There was parking underneath and the interior of each unit had been modernised, including a new kitchen, bathroom, carpet and blinds. Zac thought it the perfect place to live.

His car wasn't in his parking space. They climbed the steps to his front door, knocked several times and yelled out his name. From the path they could see his place was in darkness. Mark rang his mobile only to hear a voice message. Mark replied urgently, requesting Zac to get back to him immediately. In a few minutes, they unwillingly gave up and drove back home.

Mark kept waking during the night. Julie got up and made him a cup of tea. She hugged him and they talked for a long time until he fell into a fitful sleep.

7. Hobart

Another successful occasion was held at the Smyth's. Many generous donations were made and Imogen was, of course, admired for her style and jewellery, just as she'd hoped. Reservations by some notwithstanding, they had to admit she was a wonderful hostess and the food was to die for. A few noticed Hughe's change in demeanour but dismissed it as temporary. *He will be better when he retires,* some guests concluded.

On Monday morning, during breakfast, Imogen asked him again to divulge what was agitating him.

'Stop asking that, Immy, nothing is wrong. I'm simply a bit run down from too much work. My health will improve. Don't fuss about it.'

'Should you see a doctor?' she asked timidly.

'No!' he said loudly.

He picked up the envelope containing the donations, put it in his briefcase, gave her a quick peck on her head and hurriedly left.

She was unsure about what action to take with this growing situation. She wanted to confide with the family doctor herself but she guessed Hughe would admonish her for doing so. She did some serious thinking, pacing and hand wringing, then decided to run it by one of her closest friends instead.

Hughe came bustling into his office. An office that was a mirror image of the one in Melbourne. Luxurious and expensively furnished.

'Morning, Hughe.'

'Morning, Mick. No calls this morning please.'

'Can I just—'

His assistant was holding some folders. He had pressing enquiries he needed to pass on to his boss, but Hughe went straight into his office and closed the door.

Mick changed some appointments and took bookings from others. He had to make excuses to clients for the change, which he didn't like doing. He hated lying; to him one's integrity was paramount. This was his dream job; he didn't want to dishonour it.

Hughe surfaced from his inner office in the middle of the day and went through all the files while standing at Mick's desk.

'Come into my office, Mick, I want a word,' said Hughe. He looked haggard and serious. Mick thought this was it, he was going to be sacked.

'Have a seat, Mick.'

'Am I going to be dismissed?'

'No, no, of course not, nothing like that. I'm going to sell the practice; it's in motion as from today. I will do a handover tomorrow and the next day if needed. Johnathan Lewis will be the new owner.'

'I have to know, what happens to me?' asked Mick, who by now was thinking he was going to be out of a job.

'John has been mainly working on his own. He wants you to stay and work with him. You have a good reputation, Mick; John has promised me you will stay on. He needs someone like you. There are a few clients he will bring across so you are going to be busy. He will also work in the Melbourne office but only for two days, not three. He mainly wants to work here. It may be that he'll fold the Melbourne office. If he did, it wouldn't faze Margaret – she's retirement age. Don't say anything to her at this stage, I will talk to her about it. And another thing: you will receive a pay rise. Not immediately, say, in a month?'

'Thank you, Hughe. I'm sorry I won't be working with you but I appreciate your need to retire. I've met Johnathan a couple of times. He seems very professional and easy to talk with. I like him.'

'Good.'

They shook hands.

'I need to go to the bank now. I won't be back 'til tomorrow. See you then.'

'Right. I have a lot to do so I'll lock up as usual. See you tomorrow.' Mick was feeling pleased about his future. He excitedly rang his parents.

There were transactions Hughe needed to talk over with his bank manager. He opened a new account where funds for the sale of his practice were to be credited as well as other transfers. Then he banked the proceeds from the recent fundraiser and withdrew a large amount in cash. The bank manager was somewhat curious at some of these transactions but as they were legitimate, he was loath to ask. He had known his client for years and trusted his decisions.

Then Hughe went to see another lawyer friend of his. He needed a witness for some of his documents. With that done he went home in a much better frame of mind. Imogen was relieved. They had a chatty time through dinner; her husband was back to normal.

8. Melbourne

There was still no word from Zac. Police at the station were perplexed about his disappearance. Twenty-four hours had passed when it was decided he be declared a missing person. A bulletin was issued to police stations around Australia.

Mark reluctantly rang Zac's sister in Sydney. He didn't want to contact Zac's parents just yet.

'No. I haven't seen him for ages. He rings me now and then but not every week. I have no idea,' said Susan.

'I don't want to panic you, Sue, we'll find him. We've sent out his photo to other police stations in Australia. Someone will see him,' said Mark, in an effort to reassure her. 'It's up to you, of course, but my advice would be not to tell your parents at the moment. I know your dad's not well. No point in upsetting them just yet, not until we're sure about what's going on. Do you know if he was unhappy about anything?'

There was silence on the line for a second.

'Are you there, Sue?'

'Yes, sorry, I'm thinking. He phoned me one night. A little while ago. It was pretty late and he sounded like he'd been drinking. He said he was fed up with his job and was thinking of quitting and going bush. I thought it was just the drink. His job is his life, you know that. I think it's the reason he hasn't had any long-lasting relationships. I phoned him later from work and he was the same Zac. He had no recollection of the night before.'

'Well, that's news to me, Sue, never realised he felt like that.' Mark was dismayed at what he just heard. 'I'll keep you posted and please let me know if you see or hear anything about him.' He hung up. That settled it. Something was undeniably wrong in the life of his friend.

Mark always battled with his suspicious nature. This mindset was cultivated by the job he was devoted to. When guests had departed from an evening at their place, he would discuss his hunches. Julie often chastised him for it. 'You are so wrong about that couple. I've known them my whole life. You have nothing to prove what you are accusing them of. Stop it.'

She was right and he reprimanded himself for it. But this time he felt vindicated. Zac was in a mess, either self-inflicted or at the hands of someone else. His intuition told him so. To him, crime was ubiquitous.

Next day, Mark visited the morgue accompanied by a young constable. He wanted to know more about Jacky Zhao's death.

They stood on the other side of the glass and waved to Peter Garcia. Peter pointed at the intercom indicating Mark turn on the sound.

'Hi, Peter. What do you have for me?'

'Hello, Mark. Well, first off, he is as clean as a whistle. Healthy guy albeit slightly under weight for his height, in his twenties. Shot through the forehead, as you know. Did you find the bullet? It went through the other side. It's not here.' He pointed to Jacky's head.

'Not to my knowledge. I'll check the notes and ask the sergeant, but I'm pretty sure I'd know if it was found. Any idea of the firearm?'

'By the look of the damage to the back of the skull I would say most likely a 45-calibre bullet. Undoubtedly a handgun. We found no residue anywhere. Whoever did this knew their stuff. The place looked messy but we found nothing to help us under a microscope or chemical analysis. Jacky's forehead had been cleaned around the wound. Amazing and unusual. The amount of blood that was in that bathroom belongs to dear Jacky here. I'll finish my report today and send it to the coroner.'

'Ok, thanks, Peter. Anything about the man in the lane?'

'Ah, well, not much luck there either. We have fingerprints but nothing to match them with, same with the DNA. As I said before, he was a healthy lad, at a guess about late forties, early fifties. Clear lungs, so a non-smoker. Liver in great condition, so not a heavy drinker either. Found a splinter in his face from maybe a baseball bat or similar. Nothing of any value there as yet. I can say one thing: he wasn't circumcised so he's not from the Jewish community. Does that help?'

'No, but I wish it did,' said Mark, feeling frustrated about the lack of any evidence.

Mark admired Peter Garcia. To some he seemed nonchalant and inappropriate with some of his rather outrageous humour. But by watching Peter closely, Mark observed the respect Peter bestowed to his dead patients. There was deep compassion underneath this outwardly, irreverent individual.

He and the constable went back to the station. Mark talked to some members of the police who had completed the search at Jacky's place. He checked the notes in the file.

Nothing about a bullet. He realised how slack he'd been in not thinking about it before. But then, he expected it to still be in Jacky's skull.

He asked the sergeant and a couple of other police officers on duty to come with him to have another look over the place.

The police tapes and locked door were as they had been left. Wearing gloves and foot coverings, they slowly entered the crime scene. They repeated their search, lifting furniture, scanning the walls and ceiling of the bathroom looking for a bullet hole, opening cabinet doors and draws. An hour was spent in the tiny space Jacky had chosen as home. No bullet was found or anything else new.

Mark was on his stomach to gain a better view of cracks and indentations on the old timber floor. He reached Jacky's sofa bed and shone a torch underneath. A small bunch of dust hung around one of the support legs closest to him. He pulled it out and discovered a small cuff button within the ball of dirt. He shone his torch again and found another at the back of the bed against the wall. It was the same as the first. Both were bagged and checked against Jacky's clothing. Nothing matched but Mark decided to include them with the other bagged up pieces in the storage box. Additional notes were made to the file. Perhaps a bit methodical, *but you never know,* he thought. His optimism was rising.

9. Melbourne

It was early Saturday morning. Andrew and Rebecca were feeling lazy. They were lounging around in their dressing gowns. The smell of coffee was in the air and they were eating their way through cereal and toast while reading the paper. It was quiet except for the chirping and warbling of a magpie perched on the deck rail outside. This was their kind of bliss.

A mobile rang; it startled them. Rebecca ran to find the source of the incessant, annoying disruption to the peace. *Where did I put it?* Then she remembered; it was in the bedroom. By the time it was reached she was slightly puffed and agitated. She answered with a tone of testiness.

'Hello, hello.'

'Hello, Bec, it's Hector.'

Hector was Rebecca's second cousin. A caring man who was always there to support anyone in the family. He was adored. Rebecca's mother, Lillian, failed to appreciate her first cousin. Then again Lillian didn't appreciate anyone.

'Oh, Hector, sorry, I wasn't expecting you. Thought it might be Mum. I was in no mood to grapple with her today. Are you alright?'

"

'Bec … I heard from the aged home today. Your mum died in the early hours of the morning. She had a stroke the doctor said. Bec, Bec … are you there?'

For a moment she didn't know what to say. She never loved her mother. In a way this news was a relief. No more having to deal with her.

'Yes, yes. I'm just surprised, Hector. I was talking to her the other day, she seemed okay.'

'Yes, well, it was sudden apparently. No indication this was going to happen. A ruptured aneurysm is suspected. Anyway, she has gone to the mortuary and an autopsy will be performed, but I think the doctor suspects that as the cause. Are you able to come down? We need you here of course,' said Hector.

'Oh, of course, of course, I'll book a flight and hopefully I can be there very soon. I'll let you know the time. Can you pick me up?'

'Yes, yes, that is no bother,' said Hector. He was the only remaining relative of her deceased grandmother. A kind, gentle man loved by everyone who knew him.

Rebecca came back to the kitchen, still holding her phone.

'What's up?' said Andrew.

'Mum has died.'

He got up from his chair and folded his arms around her. 'Sorry, darling, how do you feel?' His hands were on her shoulders and he was peering into her eyes.

'Well, apart from the suddenness of it, nothing. Am I a bad person?'

'Taking into account what you have suffered, no, you are not,' said Andrew, pressing his hands on her shoulders, giving gravitas to his comment.

'I have to book a flight. I'll see if I can manage one today or early tomorrow. Will you be okay with that?' she asked.

'I'll be fine. Do what you have to do. I'll take you to the airport.' He kissed her on the cheek and let her go. She managed to make a booking for the morning flight and packed a few things.

When she arrived, Hector was waiting for her at Hobart Airport. He held Rebecca close to him, then took her arm and walked her to the car. He was just beginning to show his age. Still, his movements were as vigorous, his upright stance strong. In the main, he was in very good health.

They talked about his children and Lilly, who was still doing her volunteer work.

'She loves doing it, always has,' said Hector.

On arrival Rebecca was warmly welcomed and hugged by Lilly. She had prepared some homemade soup and bread for their dinner. With dinner finished they sat back and talked while drinking cups of tea.

'How are you feeling, Rebecca? Can we do anything for you?' asked Lilly.

'Frankly, Lilly, I don't know what to feel.' She paused for a moment. 'Perhaps a modicum of guilt. Guilt because I won't miss her, don't feel anything for her. I know that must sound dreadfully dispassionate to you, but I haven't loved my mother for a very long time.'

'We realise this, Rebecca. We knew your mother only too well. You don't have to feel any guilt,' said Lilly, while patting Rebecca's hand.

The body of Rebecca's mother was released within five days. Her death was caused by a stroke, as the doctor initially pronounced. Within a week a funeral was held at St James Anglican Church in New Town, the same church where a service was held for Harold, Lillian's father. Harold's funeral was packed with people. By contrast, there was only a sprinkling in the pews for Lillian: her strange friend, a few from the aged home, along with Rebecca, Hector and Lilly. Hector asked if she wanted to look at the body of her mother, but Rebecca didn't feel compelled to. She never wanted to see her mother again and positively not in death.

The cemetery agreed to bury Lillian with her parents, Harold and Kathleen. Rebecca felt it was the end of an era. It was her aunt and grandparents she missed the most. Not her mother.

Rebecca spent another day with Hector and Lilly. Hector showed Rebecca around his extensive, fecund garden with its plentiful flowers and vegetables.

'It reminds me of Grandpa's garden,' she said.

'Yes, I remember it well from the few visits to the Taroona house when I was younger. That's what inspired me.'

'Hector, you are the dearest person I know.'

Rebecca took his arm as they walked through the garden. The final thing he showed her was the gooseberry bush. Tears welled up and rolled down her cheeks.

'Oh dear, it wasn't meant to make you cry.' Harold was dismayed that he might have done the wrong thing altogether.

'It's fine, Hector, please. I'm very happy you have planted it. It looks healthy; you will have lovely fruit. It jolted a memory of Grandpa. I still miss him.'

'Let's go back and have a cup of tea, will we?' Hector said. Rebecca had a good sleep, much to her surprise. She longed to visited Mabel and Robert, the parents of the now deceased Tim, her first love, but they had moved to Queensland – she understood why. Hector and Lilly drove her back to the airport.

'Come and stay again, please, I miss you both very much.'

'We will,' said Lilly.

On the plane Rebecca thought about her parents. She had never heard from her father again once he abruptly left and had no idea where he was or if he were alive. As for her mother, she surmised she was gloomy about what could have been. Then, for a moment, she let herself think of Tim.

By the time the planed landed in Melbourne she had regained herself and stopped feeling so mawkish. Driving home with Andrew she realised how fortunate she was to have this loving, patient man with her.

'What's for dinner?' Rebecca cheekily asked, knowing Andrew didn't like cooking.

'Big surprise, take away,' he announced with a flourish.

'So clever, you amaze me.' Rebecca laughed.

10. Hobart

Hughe had returned to his normal self. 'He seems happier than ever,' Imogen told her friend. He was certainly in a better frame of mind. He was tidying up his affairs, which was a huge relief for him. He had reached a state of contentment.

Johnathan had gone over the financials in preparation for the takeover of the practice and found them in excellent order. They spent time reviewing outstanding legal cases. Mick, Hughe's assistant, was coming in and out of the office with cups of tea and bunches of requested files. He was looking forward to working with Johnathan Lewis.

Hughe had also made a new will with another solicitor and asked Johnathan to keep the sealed envelope containing the said will in the safe.

'Along with the will, there is a private letter in there for my wife. It's just a letter of memories and a few words to calm her if I go first,' Hughe said to Johnathan.

'I'm sure you are both going to be together for a long time to come.'

At the end of three days of sorting through files and reviewing each case, Hughe and Johnathan were sitting in the office having a whiskey each. One hundred and fifty thousand dollars had been transferred as payment for the practice and both men were very satisfied with themselves.

'What are you going to do in retirement, Hughe?' asked Johnathan.

'I think Immy and I will do a bit of travelling, around Tassie to start with. We haven't done much of that over the past few years, I've been too busy.'

'Well,' said Johnathan, taking his final gulp, 'I wish you both a very happy retirement. Don't be a stranger. I'll look forward to a lunch if you find the time. And, of course, I'll see you at one of those famous fundraisers of yours.'

They shook hands and Hughe walked out of his office. He patted Mick on the arm, they said a few words. Then he walked to the door, turned and looked back for a moment, surveying what had been his whole working life.

That evening Hughe and his wife went out to dinner with a couple of friends. Everyone had a good time. At one stage another of Imogen's friends whispered that she noticed Hughe looked much better now and Imogen happily agreed. For the next few days Imogen and Hughe travelled along the east coast of Tasmania, spending two nights at Coles Bay, where Hughe remarked, 'This has to be one of the most marvellous places on earth'. During those two nights he would stand outside for hours, looking around him, watching a sunset, listing to the sounds of lapping water or people nearby who were talking with equal appreciation and awe of the unique place.

When they returned home, some attention was paid to parts of the neglected garden and a few things around other areas of the home. They reunited with Eric and his family over dinner.

'That was a lovely night,' said Imogen as she climbed into bed, arranging her pillows and blankets.

'Yes, indeed,' said Hughe, who was already in bed reading. 'Have you taken your sleeping pill, Immy?'

'Yes, of course.'

'Good,' said Hughe. He kissed Imogen on her cheek, put down his book and turned off the bed lamp. As he lay on his side, he listened to Imogen's breathing. At the end of a half an hour he knew she was in a deep sleep. He arose from bed, put on his slippers and silently went down stairs. There were no lights on so he carefully descended the steps with the help of a torch. He went to his car, got in and quietly closed the driver's door. It was a clear moonlit night, he knew it would be, he had been studying the weather. The long, vertiginous driveway had a gradual slope. He released the handbrake then pressed lightly on the footbrake and rolled the car slowly to the front gate. When he was clear of the house, he started the car engine and turned on the headlights.

It was about two am – there was no traffic – and only about ten minutes to his planned destination. At the location he parked the car just off the road near the Royal Botanical Gardens, put on his warm, heavy, wool dressing gown – which he had previously hidden in the boot – tied the cord tightly around his waist then walked the short distance to the Tasman Bridge. He was relieved to find there was not a soul to be seen. He climbed to the highest part of the structure and looked about him, as if he were searching for something. It was a peaceful night with no wind. He looked up to the moon and over the bridge, then he jumped, out and down, feet first.

There was a gentle splash. Hughe dropped into the dark, calm, cold Derwent River. He was gone in seconds.

11. Melbourne

His mobile was buzzing. Mark looked at his clock radio. 'Christ, it's still bloody early,' he said under his breath.

Julie mumbled something inaudible while pulling the doona over her head. Mark kept running his hand over the table with his eyes closed. He located the vibrating phone and grabbed it.

'Hello,' he said, with a throat still dry from sleep.

Someone on the other end was breathing heavily.

'Hello, hello, who's this? If you don't answer I'm hanging up.'

'It's me, mate, it's Zac.'

'Zac? Where are you?'

'Oh, mate, I'm in the shit, I'm fucked,' he said. Zac's speech was thick and sluggish.

'Have you been drinking? Are you driving somewhere?'

Zac laughed. It sounded maniacal. 'Mate, I don't risk going outside at the moment.'

'Zac, tell me where you are, I'll come to you. Let me help you.'

'No go, mate, can't do that right now. I'm not in Melbourne, I had to run away.'

'Where are you?' Mark was alarmed at his friend's desperation.

'Can't tell ya. I'm going to throw this phone away now so you can't trace me, I'm moving on.' The line suddenly went dead. He'd hung up.

'Fuck.' Mark slammed his mobile down.

Julie startled awake next to him at the noise. 'What's up?'

He didn't have time to answer her question in detail – he kicked the covers away and started searching for his shoes. He needed to get to the station, trace that call as fast as he could.

'What's going on?' pressed Julie.

'It's Zac, he's not in Melbourne. Said he had to run away, I've gotta get to the station.' Mark patted his pockets, had everything he needed. He kissed Julie's forehead, creased in confusion, and headed out.

Mark was alarmed by Zac's words. He had never heard him talk like that before. He knew him to be in control and a very competent detective. The voice on the phone was nothing like that. Now, his voice sounded nervous and garbled.

A few hours went by. Zac's mobile was located in an area of South Australia. Mark punched out the numbers but it was useless. Zac had obviously done what he said he would, rid himself of the phone.

Mark contacted the South Australian police at the Adelaide station and gave them the registration number of Zac's car. For now, that was the best he could do.

12. Hobart

Imogen was woken up by something. She was still feeling the effects of her sleeping pill. What at first sounded distant was now loud and unrelenting.

'Hughe, answer the door please. Hughe!' she yelled, but he didn't answer. 'Hughe, where are you?' she repeated loudly.

She hurriedly put on her dressing gown and started down the stairs. By now she was quite irritated and intended to have a word with him for not answering the blasted, constant ringing of the doorbell. With her short-paced steps, she rushed and opened the door. By now she was panting. There were two policemen standing on the porch with their caps off and held in front of them.

'Mrs Smyth?'

'Yes.'

'This is First Constable Cliff McIntyre and I'm Senior Constable Ryan Stewart. May we come in for a moment please?'

'Yes, of course.' She hollered out again, 'Hughe, the police are here.' Imogen turned back to the constables. 'I'm sorry, I can't locate my husband at the moment,' she said with a smile, having regained her composure. 'Can I get you a cup of tea? I'm sure Hughe will be back in a minute.' She started toward the kitchen.

'Mrs Smyth, I'm sorry, but we have some bad news,' said Constable Stewart.

'Is it my son, Gary? I always worry about him travelling out there on his own. He never listens to—'

'It's about your husband.'

'Pardon?'

'Your husband. We found him this morning.'

'What? You must be mistaken. He just got out of bed, I'm sure he—'

'He was found this morning, floating in the Derwent River near Blackmans Bay Beach.' Constable Stewart was trying to humanely break the news to Imogen.

'What on earth was he doing there? I mean he does go swimming but not that far. Where is he now?'

'He's dead, Mrs Smyth, he drowned,' said the constable.

'What! Dead? My Hughe is dead? No, you're wrong he—'

'We are very sorry.'

'But he's an excellent swimmer, he couldn't have just drowned. Perhaps he hit his head or something.' Imogen was in torment. She leant against the wall in the hallway and started howling. 'No, no it can't be, no, please.' The room was spinning, she lost control of her feet.

'Let us help you to a chair.' The constables helped her to the kitchen and sat her down.

'Mrs Smyth, his car was found near the Botanical Gardens. Any idea what it was doing there?'

'No, I have no idea,' said Imogen. She felt confused and numb. 'Can you tell me anything about what happened? I don't know why he was in the river and I don't know why his car is somewhere else. He's either here, at home with me, or working. I always know where he is. Can I see him please?' she begged.

'Afraid not at the moment, Mrs Smyth. He has been taken to the morgue; an autopsy may be performed. It might give us some answers. Do you have any objection?'

'No,' Imogen said in a whisper.

'We will let you know when his body is released. Do you need someone with you? It can be arranged.' asked Constable Stewart.

'No, no, thank you. I'll, um … I will contact my son, Eric. He and his wife live close by. I also need to contact my other son, Gary. He's in the Northern Territory. He'll need to come home, he …' Imogen couldn't finish the sentence; she began sobbing again.

'Well, if you're sure, we will go now and come back when we have more news. Please accept our condolences. We will let ourselves out.'

Imogen nodded. When they were gone, she slowly walked up the stairs, gripping the handrail tightly for support. She lay down for a moment then looked over to where Hughe had slept. A depression of his body was still visible on the sheet. She howled for a time then dragged herself up from the bed and dressed. She had to tell her children.

13. Melbourne

Two weeks had passed since the body in the lane was discovered. His identity was still unknown and Mark was confounded. Solving crimes sometimes took a while, he was used to that, but this one was a puzzle. It didn't fit the usual profile. Victims of crime were frequently dumped somewhere in the bush, making it arduous trying to find them, if ever. Others were found in a dwelling or would rise to the top of a waterway and float down to somewhere. But naked, in a lane, in the middle of the city with little or no clues? That was unusual.

Mr Li had come to ask for Jacky Zhao's body so he could be sent back to China to his family.

'They want see him and other people want see him. It special time and they do special things for son, he must go back to China,' said Mr Li.

Mark was aware of the week of ceremony and ritual for the cremation of loved ones. Traditional service of the dead was immutable, the rules had to be followed. He assured Mr Li Jacky's death was being investigated thoroughly. The coroner was yet to make a finding.

'What is coroner?' asked Mr Li.

'He is a special judge, a magistrate who determines how a person died. He gets information from the doctor at the morgue. Do you understand?' Mark was trying to make the explanation as simple as he could for Li.

'No understand,' said Mr Li.

Mark requested an interpreter. Rose, a university student who provided services as an interpreter for the police at the station, arrived in an hour. Twenty minutes went by with Mr Li. Rose then confirmed he now understood. She relayed that Mr Li felt sad and worried about what happened to his nephew as he was supposed to be responsible for him. 'Jacky's parents are incensed. He said he will not be able to go back to China to visit them again.'

'Oh, I see,' said Mark. 'Unfortunately, there's nothing we can do about the situation.'

'No, I know. Mr Li told me Jacky was only twenty. His parents were hoping for a better life for him here. Jacky's mother is Mr Li's sister. No hope of reconciliation there I would think,' she said.

'So young. He seemed a happy guy, keen to learn English, good worker, I believe, and very cooperative when we questioned him. Thank you for explaining it to him, Rose,' said Mark.

Mr Li and Rose started to leave. 'I come back for Jacky,' said Mr Li.

Mark returned to his desk and went through his files. He disliked paperwork, particularly writing up reports. Even so, it was part of the job – had to be done. He ensured crimes investigated by him were meticulously recorded.

Some of the other cases he was working on were resolved. The dead teenager floating in the Yarra came about as the result of a silly, fatal decision. She had consumed copious amounts of alcohol while out with her friends and, as a dare, had jumped off the bridge into the Yarra. Everyone was pretty drunk and failed to find out if she was safe. They just went home. Mark shook his head; they just left her to it. She was identified when her parents reported her missing. Her so-called girlfriends denied any knowledge of their friends' misguided action.

The invasion of the house in Carlton had been finalised with the capture of two youths who were on drugs. They were now in jail awaiting trial. The man in the house who had received a vicious beating by the drugged-up perpetrators had recovered from his wounds and was back home. *Whether he will recover mentally is another thing. Damn drugs,* Mark thought. It was the ruin of many in the population and he couldn't comprehend it, nor had any patience for it. In his mind, they knew what they were doing right at the beginning of that treacherous trip.

He finished his paperwork, picked up his briefcase and his coat from the back of the chair. It was the end of the day shift. With a few goodbyes, he exited out the door. While walking to his car, his mobile buzzed. It was a private number.

'Hello, Mark Amos.' Silence. 'Hello, hello, Zac, is that you?'

'Yes, mate.' Zac sounded more alert and lucid this time.

'Zac, what's wrong? Tell me. Can I help?'

'No, mate, nothing you can do, I'm in real shit.'

'Let me come to you. I know you're near Adelaide somewhere. Let's talk, we can work something out.' There was a long silence. 'Zac, are you still there? If you don't want help, why are you ringing me?'

'I want to hear a familiar voice, I'm alone.' Mark could hear Zac's wretchedness.

'Listen, mate. Tell me where you are, we can meet. I won't tell anyone, I'll come alone. Just give me a place that suits you and I'll be there.'

'I'm staying at the Motor Inn — room seven, 21 Port Road, Elizabeth North. I'll see you around two o'clock tomorrow.' Zac abruptly hung up.

Mark went back in to the office and told his superior something urgent had come up, he needed to take three days leave effective immediately. There was no hesitation; it was granted.

14. Hobart

Eric and Cynthia were trying to console Imogen. From the moment they arrived, she couldn't control her feelings of grief.

'But why, why?' Imogen moaned.

'Mum, Mum, come on. We have to be strong here. There's going to be an autopsy, we will get some answers from that,' said Eric. He was kneeling down in front of her, his hands on her knees, looking up at her slumped body sitting in the kitchen chair. Her face was crumpled and red, mucus from her nose ran freely down over her chin and her eyes were coated with a watery film.

'He was happy, Eric, the happiest I've seen him for ages. I can't grasp what happened last night? Do you think he was having an affair? Oh, sweet Jesus, he was having an affair.' Imogen was convinced this imagined union contributed to his death, further increasing her despair. She resumed her loud sobbing.

'Mum! He was not having an affair. Someone in this town would know. It would have come to light by now.' Eric was trying his best to reason with her while feeling devasted himself.

Cynthia was delegated the task of answering the phone. No one knew about Hughe's death yet. But in this town word spread rapidly.

Excuses were made. 'Imogen is not feeling well, she may have the flu. No, it is not serious; no, she can't come to the phone at the moment, I'll pass on your message.' In the end, she thought it more prudent to take the phone off the hook and not answer the door unless it was the police.

'Have you tried to get in touch with Gary?' Imogen asked.

'Yes, Mum. No luck yet. You know what he's like. He could be in the middle of the desert. His satellite phone isn't answering. I'll contact his partner. If he's not with him, he may still know how to contact him.'

Cynthia had to pick up the children from school. It was decided to take them home for the moment. Eric would stay with his mother overnight.

'What do you think happened?' she asked as Eric walked her to the car.

'I have my suspicions but ... I'm not sure. I suspect he has suicided,' said Eric, trying to quell the thought himself.

'What, why do you think that?' She was trying to read his mind.

'I think it has something to do with money. Look around you, look at Mum's car, her clothes, her jewellery, the house, all of it. Dad was a successful lawyer but not that successful. Money had to come from somewhere to pay for this.'

'Have you asked Imogen if she knows anything?' she asked.

'Hmph, are you kidding? She's in a perpetual wonderland. Dad spoilt her and she lapped it up. Never questioned where the funds came from, just took it for granted.'

'This is a devastating situation, Eric. I'm so sorry.' She held him for a moment.

'I'll miss him. I loved Dad, far more than Mum. I shouldn't say that, but it's true. He worked his ass off trying to provide her every fancy, her every wish. Underneath, I find her self-indulgent and futile. Look, she took interest in us boys in her own way, but her needs came first, always.'

'That's sad, Eric.'

'It's all right. I had my music and my books and now I have you and the children. I'm so fortunate. I love you, darling. I'd better get back.' He held Cynthia close, kissed her and went back inside.

'Where have you been? I thought you had gone home with Cynthia,' said Imogen, with a look of petulance. Her eyes were now red and swollen. Gone was the sophisticated, well-groomed woman who was used to being in control. Now she seemed childlike and vulnerable. Putting his pent-up resentment aside, Eric felt sorry for her. 'We were sorting out things for the children.'

'Can you try to get hold of Gary again please, Eric? He needs to know.'

'Yes, of course.' He called again. Nothing. 'He must be out of range, Mum. I'll try ringing his partner.'

'Yes, yes, please. We have to tell him to come home,' said Imogen, who was becoming hysterical. 'He should be here!' She stamped her foot on the floor.

Eric found Richard's number. 'Hi Ric, it's Eric here. Do you know where Gary is? It's urgent … No, I can't explain at the moment but we have to get in touch with him … Right, right. Well, if he contacts you, please tell him to ring me straight away. Okay thanks.'

'Well, what's going on?' asked Imogen

'He doesn't know where he is, Mum. He's been busy with his full-time job. The last he heard Gary was going to explore some areas in the Northern Territory for his next camping expedition.'

'Oh, God.' She started to weep again.

Eric cooked a basic omelette for his mother. She managed to eat some of it only to throw it back up in the toilet. He sat with her while she had a cup of black tea then gave her one of her sleeping pills and took her upstairs. He tucked her into bed and sat with her until she fell asleep.

Satisfied his mother was in a deep sleep, he poured a brandy, went back into the kitchen, sat down and tried to think of what went wrong with his father. Nothing was adding up. Hughe had always seemed happy. As a lawyer he was never short of clients. He was also an admired and trusted member of the community. His wife was faithful and supportive, notwithstanding much of it was for her own interests. However, it meant she was always by his side. Eric was a rationalist; in his mind his father had committed suicide and it was either because he was dying from some disease or he owed money. It couldn't be anything else.

Imogen woke up next morning, slowly emerging from the fog of a sleeping drug. The realisation of Hughe's death swiftly returned, like an unexpected punch to the head. Her husband had gone; her life would never be the same. She started to howl. Eric, who had had a fretful three hours sleep, ran up the stairs to her.

'Oh, Eric, I can't accept it, I can't accept it.' Imogen was becoming more frantic.

'Mum, Mum, you have to, Dad is gone. You will feel lost and bereaved but we are here for you. We will have to deal with this one day at a time.'

'That's fine for you,' she said with a tone of resentment. 'You're young; you have Cynthia and the children. What do I have now?'

'I'm going to ask the doctor and a member of the church to come and see you. They may be able to help you through your grief, Mum.'

Eric organised for both of them to come and be with her. Imogen got out of bed, showered and dressed. She applied some makeup in an attempt to look a bit better for her visitors.

Johnathan Lewis contacted Eric and asked if he could come to the office for a moment at around two pm. He asked him not to say anything to Imogen.

A Reverend from the Church of England and the family doctor arrived almost at the same time. Eric asked the Reverend if he could stay with his mother until he got back. 'I won't be long.'

'Take your time,' said Reverend Bennett.
Mick, Hughe's former assistant, came around his desk to the front door to greet Eric.

'I'm so sorry about your dad, Eric. I liked him. He was a great boss.'

'How did you know?' Eric asked.

'The police were here enquiring. They didn't say much, just that he was deceased. What happened?'

'We don't know, Mick, we're as mystified as you.' Mick gave him a sympathetic hug.

Johnathan stepped out of his inner office and welcomed Eric. 'Come in, Eric.'

Eric entered the place where his father had sat for many years. He had to control the tears that threatened to flow.

'Our deepest sympathy, Eric.' Johnathan enclosed both of his hands over Eric's. 'Please, have a seat. Do you know what happened?'

'Only as much as you, I think. They found him floating in the river near the beach at Blackmans Bay, then they found his car parked near the Botanical Gardens. Frankly, and this must stay in the room, I suspect he suicided. But I just can't figure out why. I'm totally in the dark,' said Eric.

'Well, that's why I've asked you to come in. It's not the proper way to do things, but your father has made a will. It has been kept in the safe here as he directed. Included with that, apparently, there is a letter in there for your mother. Now, we don't know how he died yet, but we both have our qualms about this. Under the circumstances I would suggest you read it first. It may contain something that could unsettle her more. If I may say so, I've been to most of their social functions and I've summed up your mum as being, well, susceptible. I hope I haven't offended you and, indeed, this is your decision,' said Johnathan.

'On the contrary, I think you are very perceptive. I would like to read that letter. I don't need to see the will. Can it be put it into a separate sealed envelope? She wouldn't know. Perhaps you could take the will and give it to her in person, next week maybe? Moreover, the letter may not be as damaging as we think,' said Eric.

'If you're sure, it can be organised. I'll get it out now. I'd rather you not say anything to Mick about our little arrangement. He's a stickler for proper process,' said Johnathan with a brief grin.

'Not a word,' said Eric.

In a few moments Johnathan returned. He handed the envelope to Eric. 'Would you like to be alone?' he asked.

'I'd like you to stay, if you can. Do you have any more clients today?'

'No, I'm clear. I have some writing up to do. I'll focus on that while you're reading.'

Eric tentatively opened the large envelope that contained the will. Another DL-envelope was sitting beside it with its flap conveniently folded down inside so the reader didn't need to tear it open. *That's Dad, always thoughtful.* He took a minute to collect himself. He was about to read his father's words that were meant for his mother. This letter could be a very private, intimate thing between a married couple who had been together for over forty years. Was he doing the right thing? This wasn't what his father wanted. He would be outraged. Eric sat for a good five minutes, thinking. Ultimately, he was convinced vetting this letter was to save his mother from more pain. On the other hand, it may not have anything disquieting in the content. There was only one way to determine it.

He delicately unfolded the parchment paper on which Hughe had written, in his trademark neat style, a message for Imogen.

My Dearest Immy,

I write this letter to you with a heavy heart. By now you will doubtless be in a state of excruciating anguish and bewilderment at my actions. Believe me when I say I loved you from the moment we met and that love never faded, ever. But things couldn't go on the way they were. As I write I am feeling ashamed and dammed. I have done some very silly things and have taken the coward's way out by leaving you, dear Immy, to carry my burden.

I wanted to give you your every desire, to make you as happy as I possibly could. It was an endless joy to see you shine, confident and be the best of the best. Of course, if I am honest, it wasn't just that. Because, making you the most alluring and confident person in the room reflected back to me. It made me feel proud, gave me more status and maybe envied by my peers. This was vanity at its most extreme and it was my undoing. You, dear Immy, are blameless, I want you to know that. This is entirely my doing.

I was entrusted with someone's ill-gotten cash. I knew its source was from drugs but I was paid well to invest it for them. To clean it up, so to speak. Make it look legal, if you will. At first, I did as directed, but I became too tempted. I spent the money made on those investments, then I began to spend the money from the initial cash invested by my client. I used to present false statements to prove how their cash had grown. I made my own nightmare. There came a time when they demanded the whole balance of their money back. They needed it, they said. Of course, I just didn't have it. I was threatened, my life was in danger. So, I borrowed and with that money and funds from the sale of my practice I have managed to pay most of it back. However, I had to raise a loan against the house to do it. I know you will find it impossible to absolve me for this. Your magnificent house will have to be sold to pay the loan back to the bank, Immy, along with the car and perhaps some of your elegant jewellery. There is a minimal amount in one account that has been paying some of the loan back, thus far, but it won't last long. You will have to see the bank manager to attain how much is left in that account and obtain the services of a real estate agent, promptly.

As I said, I have taken the coward's way out. I couldn't face people; I couldn't face the shame it would bring. But much more than that, I couldn't face you with this truth.

I hope you will, one day, forgive me.

Please tell our sons I love them.

Your loving,

Hughe

Upon reading the letter, Eric bent over in the chair. His head was throbbing. He suspected it might be a money problem, but this? This was far more nerve-wracking. His father had been using drug money. He looked up at Johnathan, who had been startled by Eric's reaction.

'You look pale, Eric. Can I get you some water?'

'Yes, please.' Eric was feeling sick.

'Mick, bring in some water for Eric, please?' he asked through a partially opened door. Mick brought in a glass then closed the door behind him.

'Do you want to talk about it?' asked Johnathan.

Eric took a large gulp of the water, he paused then, 'I want you to read it. I would welcome your advice. At this stage I simply don't know what to do.'

'If you're sure,' said Johnathan.

Eric handed it to him. He sat quietly, swigging water as Johnathan read the contents of the letter meant for Imogen's eyes only. The lawyer raised his eyebrows and they stayed that way until he finished.

'Phew, well, this is very serious. I must admit to being stunned. Hughe? Drug money? How could he be so stupid?'

'Any ideas, Johnathan? I can't think.' Eric felt thoroughly dejected.

'My first thought is the bank. We need to look at the will first though,' said Johnathan.

'Do you think we should?'

'Definitely. I need to know something before you proceed.'

The will was only two pages long. Johnathan studied the pages painstakingly. 'Right, good, he's made you the executor.'

'What? I don't know what to do as executor. Why did he do that?' said Eric.

'It's okay, I'll help you.' Johnathan read out some of Hughe's instructions. 'The house is already in Imogen's name, as is her car. There is some money in the bank, but not much apparently. He said you and Eric can take anything you want from the house. Imogen is to keep her jewellery but may have to sell some of it. Most importantly, the house must be sold to pay off the loan. Eric and Gary are to either find her alternative accommodation or have her live with them. There is also a few thousand in a superannuation account. There's a couple of other things, but that's the gist of it.' He handed Eric the will. 'Look, you don't have a death certificate yet, do you?'

Eric's phone rang. 'Eric speaking … Right, yes, yes, of course. I will go there now. Thank you. That was the police, Johnathan. They're at Mum's place. The minister is still with her. Dad has to be officially identified. Mum doesn't want to see him like he is so I will. Police will meet me there.'

'Right. Look, at this stage, I would advise not saying anything to your mother just yet. Go to the morgue first. Would you like me to accompany you?'

'Yes, please Johnathan. I'll go now and wait for you there.'

Eric was grateful for Johnathan's company. He trusted him just as his father had. And he needed the help. Sometimes he felt completely at a loss.

Johnathan arrived in a few minutes behind Eric. Along with a police officer, the men entered the morgue. Signatures were given. They were taken in to view the deceased.

Hughe's face was sunken. His formerly pink skin had changed to the colour and texture of white chalk. He looked nothing like the healthy father Eric remembered. Deathly white took on a realistic meaning for him now. He looked at him lying there, at peace. Tears streamed down his face.

He always loved and looked up to his father and wished, with his whole being, this hadn't happened. What surprised Eric was how stupid and desperate his father had become – whatever was he thinking?

A few quiet minutes passed, then he confirmed it to be his father, Hughe Smyth. The pathologist said Hughe must have carried something heavy on his person, perhaps in the pockets of his thick dressing gown. The items would ensure he sank but they found nothing to prove it. Whatever the case, his body was set free to float up to the top.

'Would he have been dead by then?' Eric asked.

'Undoubtedly,' said the pathologist.

With a few words of condolence, the officer left.

'I've been thinking. How about you go home now and come back to the office tomorrow. We'll work out some items to deal with first,' said Johnathan.

'Yes, I agree, I have to get back to Mother. About ten?' asked Eric.

'Suits me. See you then.'

'Thank you, Johnathan, I appreciate this more than I can say.'

Eric was slowly driving home. He couldn't rid the image of his father drowning. Did he struggle at the last minute? Did he change his mind? Was he in agony? *We'll never know,* he thought. A car tooted behind him. He looked up; he hadn't been concentrating and had stopped in the middle of the road. Startled he sped up.

The minister was still with Imogen when Eric arrived.

'I'm so sorry to keep you,' said Eric.

'Not at all. I'll come by tomorrow, Mrs Smyth,' said the Reverend. When he'd left, Eric and Imogen went to the kitchen. She seemed calmer.

'Cynthia and the children are coming over shortly. She's bringing some fish and chips,' said Imogen, trying to smile.

'I saw Dad, Mum.'

'I know, I just couldn't bring myself to—'

'I understand, Mum.' He held his mother while she wept on his shoulder.

'I'm going to make a cup of tea. I need to do something,' she said while wiping her eyes.

The family sat together at the kitchen table trying to eat. The children talked to each other quietly, the adults ate in silence.

When dinner was finished, the children were sent to watch television while the adults discussed matters.

Imogen decided to confide in her best friend. She wanted her to come and stay over if she could. Cynthia thought it better if she came and stayed with them. In the end that suggestion was viewed the wisest. Imogen went upstairs to pack a suitcase.

'Have you been able to get in touch with Gary yet?' Cynthia asked Eric in a low voice.

'No, nothing. If we don't hear from him in the next couple of days, I'm going to ask if the Northern Territory police can try to find him. He has to come home.'

'Yes. He has to know about your farther and you shouldn't have to deal with this on your own.'

Thirty minutes had passed before Imogen was ready. Cynthia drove her and Eric took his mother's car back to their home. He wasn't confident about this arrangement. His mother was a capricious woman, but what other choice did he have?

The spare room was set up to make Imogen comfortable, restful and safe. She had been given two sleeping pills only

– one for each night. It was a cautionary measure from the family doctor. They watched her take one and kept checking her until she was asleep.

'Are you sure she's asleep?' Eric asked.

'Yes, definitely.'

'Right. I have something to tell you,' he said.

15. Adelaide

'I'm not happy about this, Mark. You have no idea what you're walking into.'

Julie had a sixth sense, a feeling of dread about him going. She trusted her sixth sense. It rarely visited her, but when it did, it was invariably right.

'Darling, I've encountered far more dangerous situations than this. Come on, this is my friend you're talking about. We've been friends forever. I trust him with my life,' said Mark, while focusing on the packing of his overnight bag. He stood up straight and looked into her eyes. 'I'll be very watchful.' He leaned towards her, held her face and kissed her. She never tired of the thrill of his mouth on hers. Both felt aroused. For a moment nothing else mattered. They wanted each other instantaneously.

'No time for that now,' said Mark, carefully guiding each other apart with a feeling of sexual frustration. He wanted her more than anything at this moment. 'We need to go,' he said, dragging himself away.

Julie drove Mark to the airport. She couldn't shake her feeling of unease.

'Do you have your gun?' she asked.

'Of course not. Can you imagine going through security?'

'But you can show your ID, surely.'

'For one, it would hold me up with the explaining I would have to do and, most importantly, I don't need it.'

'If you say so.' Julie was not convinced. She kissed him goodbye, watched him walk to the doors, waved, then drove home. Tonight, would be a sleepless one. She wouldn't rest until he was back tomorrow.

Mark took a flight that landed in Adelaide at one-forty pm. He grabbed a taxi – in twenty minutes he was at the address Zac gave him. It was a very old '60s style motel that had seen better days. He knocked on the door of unit seven and observed Zac's dusty car parked nearby.

Zac opened the door, barely. When he saw it was Mark, he let him in, quickly closing it behind him. He briefly held his friend. 'Christ, am I glad to see you,' he said.

The room was decorated with brown and yellow wallpaper, some of it faded and peeling. The bed was covered with a quilt in the same washed-out colours. There was a square table with one worn chair, along with a bedside table holding a dirty looking lampshade. The whole place smelt of stale cigarettes and discarded takeaways.

The formerly well-groomed Zac now looked unkempt. His hair was greasy and plastered down onto his skull. His normally white, smooth face was blotched and unshaven and his clothes wrinkled and stained. He had a packed, scruffy bag by the door. 'In case I have to make a quick getaway,' he said.

'What the hell has happened to you?' Mark was staggered by the change in demeanour of his friend.

Zac sauntered over to the old fridge and pulled out a beer. 'Do you want one?'

'Sure,' said Mark, hoping this would relax his friend.

'Cheers,' said Zac.

The men clinked their beer bottles together. They took a few swigs, nothing was said. Zac sat in the chair with his head down, nervously tearing at the beer bottle label. Mark sat on the edge of the bed, waiting for the explanation to begin.

Mark spoke first. 'Zac, I came here to help you, my best friend, my trusted mate. The one I rely on when we're out there facing some of the worst. Come on, tell me.'

'You're right, you're right.' Zac was shaking his head. 'And I've blown it.'

'Whatever it is, we can face it together. How can I help you? What can I do?' said Mark.

Zac went to the fridge for another beer.

'Do you need another, Zac?'

'Hey! Mate, this stuff is the least of my worries.'

Mark was becoming exasperated. 'Zac, if you're not going to tell me, I may as well go back home. I have an apprehensive, loving wife waiting for me. She didn't want me to come here in the first place. Spit it out.'

'Okay, okay,' Zac barked. 'This is not easy. Telling you is very, *very* hard,' he said with emphasis. 'You're lucky: you have a gorgeous wife, a great dad, mother and stepmother as well. You have good friends, including me. You get along with the work guys, they like you. Then there's me. I don't have any of it. I'm not that popular. I don't have a beautiful woman to go home to. My work is my life. End of story.' Zac was pacing while taking swigs from the bottle. 'It can get pretty lonely, I can tell you,' he said, pointing his index finger at Mark.

'I think that's crap, Zac, you—'

'I haven't finished,' Zac said loudly. 'Sometimes I would go to the odd pub or club for company. One time I met a guy. He was interesting so we talked and drank. Over time we'd occasionally meet up there. I thought he must have been as lonely as me. He told me he worked in insurance. I lied and told him I was an accountant. Telling anyone you're a cop can turn people off. The whole thing seemed legit, you know? I trusted him. One night he invited me to a party at someone's place. So, I went along, nothing to lose. The place was swinging, drinks, good music, good-looking women. I drank a bit too much that night. He invited me into another room and, well, some were snorting. I could tell it was heroin. He asked if I wanted some. I said no at first. "Go on", he said. "It will take the loneliness away." So, I did. It was only now and then at first but, as you know, it's an addictive habit. Over time I needed more, more often. It was sending me broke. To pay for it I recently stole two kilos of the stuff from my dealer. I knew where he stashed it. I had to break into his place though. He didn't see me do it but he knew I was desperate enough. He'll send his thugs to get me. He wants it back. It's worth thousands.'

'Jesus, Zac. How on earth did you let yourself get into this mess? You know about drugs and its effects. Christ, it's part of the job,' said Mark.

'Don't bloody lecture me, mate, okay? Don't.' Zac pointed his finger right at Mark's face.

'Sorry, sorry. It's, well … I'm astounded. I didn't expect this. Come back with me, Zac. We'll sort it out, we'll protect you.' Mark stood up to go to Zac. Then he felt a thud to his jaw sending him backwards onto the bed. Zac had hit him and was now pointing a gun right at his chest.

'I'm not going anywhere with you. You can't help me. There is nothing you can do about this mess. It was a mistake asking you to come here. Don't move, if you do, I promise, I will bloody well shoot you. Don't try and follow me either. I have plans to disappear, you won't find me.'

Zac was walking backwards to the door. He grabbed his bag while keeping the gun pointed at Mark; he didn't take his eyes off him. Then he sprinted out the door to his car. Before Mark could make a move, the car screeched away at speed.

The detective in Mark launched him into action. He hesitated for a few seconds. No, he had to do it. He notified the local police and gave them a description of the car – he would be there shortly to give more facts. But first, he went to reception. Zac hadn't signed in as Zac Harris.

'Nope. Don't know anything about the guy in seven. He paid in cash for the first week but not for the last couple days. He's asked for an extension. Said he'd pay me today.'

Mark paid the man for the outstanding amount. Then he arranged for a cab to take him to the station.

Mark sat with the detective senior sergeant and relayed the whole story about his once trusted friend Zac Harris.

'Right. Disastrous situation. I know how you must feel. We need the Feds on this as well. We'll find him.'

'Thanks, Senior Sergeant. I can't do anything more here now, so I'll go back to Melbourne. You have my contacts. Thank you for your help.'

They shook hands and Mark caught a cab to the airport. He contacted Julie to pick him up. He was scheduled to arrive at six-thirty pm. She was glad he was coming back home.

'No, I can't tell you now. I'll explain when I see you. Love you,' said Mark.

Once on the plane he had time to think. His trusted friend had pointed a gun at him and was willing to shoot. This was unimaginable, irresolvable and it sat heavily with Mark. He was now having mixed, painful thoughts about his colleague. Zac was in the grip of an insidious drug. It had a pernicious effect on his life; he was now spiralling out of control. 'Fucking drugs,' Mark said to himself.
Julie kissed and hugged him when he arrived.

'My love, I will never doubt your sixth sense again,' he said.

On the drive home he told her what had happened.

'You're lucky to be alive, Mark. God, Zac's life is now a mess. He's in the grip of drugs. He's no longer the man we once knew,' Julie said, as they alighted from the car.

'Yep, I know. I hope they find him. If not, it's likely he could get killed.' He was very perturbed about his friends decline. Exhaustion came over Mark. Zac's unexpected strike to the left side of his face and jaw was becoming more painful. And the threat of being shot now began to replay over and over in his head. Inside, he was shaking.

'There's a bruise there now,' said Julie. 'Let me take you to the doctor right now.'

'I'm okay, darling. No headaches, blurry vision or nausea.'

Mark slumped in a chair while Julie tended his wound. 'I will go to the doc in the morning, but first, I need to sleep, I'm spent.'

'Let's get you into bed.' Julie held him around his waist and helped him to the bedroom.

16. Hobart

Cynthia was able to keep her mother-in-law occupied. It was school holidays and the children were home. Occasionally, Imogen would scurry into her room when Hughe's death invaded her consciousness again and she needed to cry in private. Eventually she would emerge, wiping her eyes, and re-join in the children's activities or help around the house. She insisted on cooking, which suited her daughter-in-law who didn't enjoy the culinary part of her domestic duties.

There was a lot to do relating to Hughe's death. The coroner had yet to make a finding. Eric had applied to be the senior next of kin, explaining his mother was not in a fit state to be receiving updates. This was accepted and he would be the main contact from now on. Under Johnathan's guidance he also applied for an interim death certificate. The bank confirmed they would accept it. They understood it was crucial.

Eric was in Johnathan's office.

'What did the coroner's office say?' asked Johnathan.

'Another two to three days. They don't think there are any suspicious circumstances,' said Eric. 'Johnathan, I need to know about your fees for your time and help here. I have some funds put away but … well …?'

'Pro bono,' said Johnathan. 'My admiration and respect for your father hasn't diminished. Moreover, he would want me to do this for you.'

'Thank you, Johnathan.'

'You're more than welcome. I have a client coming shortly. Do you think this would be a good time to go in person for the interim certificate?' asked Johnathan.

'Yes, they said I could. When I have that I'll go to the bank. I'll take the will with me too. I need to talk to Mother. I'm not going to tell her the whole story. I'll keep you posted. May need to see you tomorrow but I'll let you know,' said Eric.

'Good, right. Let me know. Wishing you the best, Eric.' Eric waited an hour before he received the certificate and with it went straight to the bank. It was imperative he establish the financial position.

'I'm sorry about your father, Eric. I suspected something was wrong with him. Taking out a loan against the house was something I never thought I'd see. He also drew out a lot of money in cash,' said the bank manager.

'Do you know why?' Eric enquired.

'No idea, I'm afraid. I wasn't privy to that information. I did ask but he wouldn't divulge it. There's enough in one account to make another two months worth of loan payments. Then, well, that's it. Now, he did open another account with a few thousand. He gave me explicit instructions for this. It has to be put in your name but I need identifications and your signature.'

When the necessary bank specifics were done, Eric walked out feeling, to some degree, relieved. He missed having his brother by his side during this ordeal. Though he had

Johnathan's support, the weight of decision-making and filling out endless forms was taking its toll. His emotions were raw and he missed his father. He wondered how long Hughe had carried this liability. *Why didn't he seek help, tell someone?* He called Richard.

'Hi Ric, it's Eric here. Any news about Gary?'

'No, sorry, Eric. I went round to his place. It's shut up and it looks like he hasn't been there for a while. There was mail in his letterbox. No answer on his phone either. The phone sounds dead. Look, it's not unusual for him to go away for a few weeks. The strange thing is his Land Rover is still there. He could be travelling with someone of course; he's done that once before.'

Eric felt he had to inform him about Hughe. 'This is strictly confidential, Ric. It's for Gary's ears only.'

'Oh, Eric, that is a tragic thing to happen. I'm very sorry to hear this. Perhaps you can get in touch with the Northern Territory police and see if they would execute a search. I can give them an idea of some of the places he might be, if you like.'

'Yes, I'll do that. Thanks for helping, Ric, I appreciate it. He has to come home. Bloody big place to be searching for someone, but hopefully they'll find him.' Eric was beginning to feel something was wrong. A hundred things went through his mind in an instant. An accident, vehicle break down, lack of water or an attack by someone. He could be lying out there, in the desert somewhere, injured or dead. 'Okay, well, Ric, if you hear anything please let me know, day or night. I'll contact the police now.'

Eric went to the local police station and told them about the turn of events and his missing brother. They would contact the Northern Territory police and ask for a search to be organised. The sergeant agreed with Eric. Gary may be stuck out there somewhere. Richard's knowledge would help.

On his way home, Eric was determining what was appropriate to tell his mother. He wouldn't alarm her about Gary just yet. He would give her the will but not the letter. He would talk her through some of its contents. Hopefully she wouldn't ask him to expand on it.

Eric's girls interrupted the Monopoly game they were having with their grandmother to greet their father with hugs.

He and Cynthia had started a family later than most. The girls came a year apart; one was now in year seven and the other in year eight at the same secondary college. They had always been biddable children. Their parents hoped this would continue through the puberty and teenage years. 'Fingers crossed,' they once said to each other.

Cynthia came into the room and held him for a moment. She noticed he looked drawn and pale.

'Cup of tea, coffee, beer?' she asked.

'All of the above,' he said with a wry grin.

She knew this I need help expression well. 'A beer would be best then I think,' she said.

'How are you, Mum?' he asked.

'Terrible, awful. Can you give me any idea of what's happening? When can I see Hughe? I need to see him.' She looked pleadingly at her son.

'Let's have dinner first and when the girls are in their rooms, we can talk about it. What's for dinner? It smells like a roast.'

'Imogen is cooking tonight, she wanted to,' said Cynthia, handing Eric a beer and a look that said, 'Don't say anything'.

Dinner wasn't quite as solemn this time. It was important to the family they keep the atmosphere normal, if that was feasible. Imogen served everyone and made an effort not to break down. The girls talked and the others joined in. They spoke about a range of subjects but nothing about Hughe and his demise. Imogen picked at her food. When the dishes were cleaned up and the girls were occupied with studying, Eric sat with his mother and Cynthia and told Imogen what he knew at this stage. He left out information he deemed necessary for his mother's peace of mind.

'The coroner hasn't released his body yet, Mum. I was told it will be another couple of days. I've been to see Johnathan. Dad's will was kept in the safe there. I have briefly read it and—'

'Well, I want to look at the will, Eric, he was my husband. Give it to me.' She snatched it from him.

There was silence as Imogen read Hughe's instructions. Her face turned red. 'I have to sell the house, my jewellery and my car. Why? What is going on? Why has he done this to me? And he's put you in charge?' Imogen was shouting. 'He always took care of me, now he's left me with a mess. Why do I have to sell up all we owned?' She re-read parts of the will again.

'Mum, I know you must be—'

'I'm furious, furious. I'm in mourning, as if that's not enough, now I know I'm going to lose my most precious things. I loved what I had. Did he spend the lot or what?'

They tried to calm her. She pushed them away.

'Apparently he had some money problems so he took out a loan against the house,' said Eric, handling his mother tactfully.

'Where am I going to live? What about my things? What about my friends, my beautiful house? I can't tell them Hughe stuffed up, can I? Oh my god.' Imogen had now reached a hysterical state.

'Calm down, Mum. It looks bad now, but we will sort this out together. Please, take your sleeping pill. Let's talk about what to do after the funeral.'

It took some convincing but, in the end, Imogen took her medication and fell asleep.

'Where the hell is Gary?' asked Cynthia. 'We need him here.'

They were sitting in their lounge room, speaking in whispers.

'I've requested help from the Northern Territory police to do a search. Ric said he'll give them an idea of some of the places he might be. His Land Rover is still in the garage. I'm not telling Mum about this yet. Things are becoming even more alarming and so fucking complicated.'

'We're going to have to tell her, Eric.'

'I know but not yet. Not 'til Dad is buried. I'm not going to tell her about Dad's questionable transactions until the house is sold and we can find somewhere for her to live. I don't what her to live here. It wouldn't work; she's too fractious. I can't entertain the thought of her being in our home.'

'I'm glad you said that,' she said while pulling him to her. He put his head on her shoulder.

17. Melbourne

Mark's face and jaw were cleared of any serious damage. Damage to his equilibrium was another matter. He would oscillate from sympathy, fear, anger and shock. The more he thought about it, the more heartbroken he became about Zac's downfall and the threat he'd made.

He'd called his superior and filled him in. The Melbourne police station had been notified by South Australian police that Zac was still missing; they would continue searching for him.

'Okay. Come in and write up your report then take your other days off. We'll let you know if anything happens,' said the detective sergeant.

Mark felt rested from his days away and was eager to get back to the station. He went through Zac's files, which, in many instances, mirrored his own except for the cases he was working on with other colleagues. Nothing emerged that gave any clues. He had taken the odd day off, which now, in hindsight, was in all probability due to his drug habit.

The dead man in the lane still hadn't been identified and was now lying in refrigeration at the morgue.

Investigations were ongoing for Jacky Zhao's death. As he had been identified, Mark focused on this crime first. He was sitting at his desk making notes when the detective sergeant beckoned him in to his office.

'They've found Zac. Alive but in a rough state. He was hiding in the Woorabinda Bushland Reserve. They found his car first and started walking through the bush. He was asleep apparently. Caught him by surprise, he didn't resist though. Can't believe he just left his car in the car park. Surely he'd know we'd find it.'

'Perhaps he didn't care about being found. Well, at least he's alive,' said Mark, relieved, regardless of Zac's of attack on him.

'Yes. He'll be extradited, of course. His car will be towed back. That's going to cost him plenty. We'll bring him in here for an investigation. You will be brought in as a witness. Do you want to file a complaint about his attack on you?'

'No, I don't want to file a complaint. I'm still finding it tough coming to terms with the way he's turned out like this. How could it happen?' Mark was still incredulous at Zac's fall from grace.

'The nature of drugs is a curse around the world. It can happen to anyone. I'm sorry about Zac, I know you were close.'

'Not anymore.' Mark sighed heavily. 'Thanks for your thoughts.'

It was late afternoon when Mark saw Zac being taken to an interview room with two members of the drug squad. He looked like he'd cleaned himself up. He was wearing his best blue jacket. The sight of Zac wearing part of the same clothes he had worn on the day he and Julie were married made him feel despondent.

A few hours passed then Zac left and Mark was taken to another room. He then relayed to the investigating officers' specifics of what happened on that day and referred them to his report. He confirmed he didn't see any drugs before or on that day.

'We can't charge him with possession at this stage,' said the officer. 'We've searched his car and his home. We've found nothing. He has handed in his gun and ID and he's gone back home. He acknowledges he is no longer a member of the police force. There's going to be an internal investigation into the whole episode.'

'I suspect he's dumped the drugs or hidden them somewhere. He must have had them at some stage because he was petrified someone was coming for him,' said Mark.

'We'll keep an eye on him from a distance for a while,' said the officer. 'Are you intending to contact him again?'

'No, I don't trust him now. Not sure what he's capable of.'

'If you change your mind and you find out anything, we are very keen to know about it.'

'Of course,' said Mark.

Days later Mark and Julie were relaxing at home, curled up on the couch watching a movie. His mobile buzzed. He didn't recognise the number.

'Mark Amos.'

'Mark, it's Zac. I know what I did to you was pretty ordinary. We were mates and I'm feeling low about it. I wondered if I could buy you a drink and have a talk?'

'I don't know, Zac. Are you off the drugs?'

'Yep, I'm clean. I've started going to rehab.'

Mark hesitated, then, 'What about Thursday night, seven o'clock at the Royal?'

'Thanks, mate, see you then.'

Julie sat up. 'Are you serious? You're going to meet him – are you mad?'

'I want to know more. Who is his supplier? What did he do with the two kilos? He was so frightened he had to run away and yet he's now back living in the same residence. It doesn't add up.'

'Will you have some sort of back up?' she asked.

'He's not going to shoot me in public, Julie. Don't forget, he's handed in his gun and he's off the drugs at the moment. I'll be fine. Why? Is your sixth sense saying something?' He tickled her and she playfully punched him in the arm.

On Thursday Mark arrived to find Zac sitting at the bar. It wasn't the usual warm greeting. Mark ignored Zac's extended hand.

'You're beginning to look better than the last time I saw you,' said Mark, taking a seat.

'I'm clean now, makes a difference. What would you like to drink?'

'Just a beer, thanks.'

For a moment, neither said anything; instead, they studied the large boisterous crowd, while intermittently putting a bottle to their mouths to take a swig. There was the satisfied smacking of lips as they wiped away any beer residue with their sleeves.

'I'm truly sorry, mate,' Zac said.

'What's going on with you?' asked Mark, disregarding his apology. 'Where's the drugs? Why aren't you frightened anymore? Last time I saw you, you were afraid for your life.'

'Fine, fine. Obviously, you don't want our friendship any longer,' said Zac.

'Can you blame me? You were ready to kill me. You were out of your mind.'

'I wasn't going to shoot you; it was just a threat. How many times can I say sorry? I deeply regret it, okay?'

Mark calmed down but remained suspicious. 'Right, okay, okay. What did you do with the drugs, Zac?'

'Oh, right, so that's why you came to see me. You want information, not mateship.'

'We can't be like we were, Zac. I believed in you without question. That's gone. You must understand that.'

'Yeah, yeah, all right.' Zac slumped further down on his stool and leaned on the bar.

Mark felt the return of pain and loss about the man who was once his long-time, trusted partner. 'Just tell me what has happened between then and now,' Mark said in a conciliatory tone.

'I drove away but not far. I hid and watched the unit. You came out and went to reception, then caught a taxi. I went back to the unit and hid the drugs in the toilet cistern. I contacted my supplier and told them where the drugs were hidden and they needed to get someone to pick them up. I warned them if I had a hint they were trying to get me, I would tell the police. They've backed off; they had what they wanted. I then drove to the lovely reserve and walked around. I was so bloody tired. I just laid down and went to sleep.'

'Are you sure you're safe now? What's stopping them from coming to get you?' asked Mark.

'Because I've been caught by the police and because I've threatened them with telling the cops, they're not going to risk it. Anyways, I'm not worth their attention.'

'Who's your supplier, Zac?'

'Ah, now that's why I'm not worth their attention anymore. They know I will never give you anything,' said Zac, pointing with his index finger.

'I wouldn't count on that, Zac. You're dealing with dangerous people. You stole from them; they're not going to forget it. There is no honour amongst these bloody bastards. They're corrupt criminals, you know that. Tell me who your dealer is, we can protect you.'

'No go, mate, never. Can we change the subject?' said Zac.

Mark quit the questioning for now. It was not going anywhere. He sighed heavily. 'One good thing is you look and sound much better. I hope for your sake it stays that way. How's the money situation? What are you going to do for work?'

'Money is very low. I have a month's pay and some super but I have to find something. Maybe as a private investigator or a bouncer. I'd be good at both of those.'

Mark wasn't convinced. Zac lived for the police force. It was in his DNA.

'You're wearing the same jacket you wore at our wedding.' Mark felt the jacket and stroked the sleeve closest to him.

'Yeah, I always liked it. The pants don't fit anymore though. How's Julie?'

They had another beer and reminisced about past days.

'I'd better get going, Zac. We'll have another beer sometime. Stay off that stuff.'

They shook hands. Zac stayed on and ordered another beer.

Mark was sitting in his car, thinking about their meeting. He noticed something about Zac. It was a long shot but it warranted further scrutiny.

18. Hobart

The coroner had brought down his findings. Hughe Smyth had suicided; there were no suspicious circumstances.

The decision was made to hold a private funeral, family only. A notice was posted in the paper, which prompted cards and flowers. Most were sent to Imogen's house. She would wander around looking into the rooms, remembering her life with Hughe. Sometimes she'd weep, other times she would be wrathful and confounded. She was forlorn at the loss of her husband and broken about losing her house along with her status in society. Life would never be the same; she wanted to keep out of sight.

Back at Eric's house, the many flowers were put in vases and a list of names was started – a reference for when thank you cards needed to be sent.

Hughe was cremated according to his wishes. His ashes would be interred into the cavity of one of the brick walls standing at the Cornelian Bay Cemetery. A plaque would be placed over the sacred space with a written record of his name and that of his surviving family. Ironically, his particular spot would be facing the Tasman Bridge.

Gary wasn't present at the service; he was still missing and the family were agonising over his absence.

'Something has happened to him. I just feel it. It's unlike him not to ring me by now,' said Imogen.

'You know what he's like, Mum. He's in his own universe, he sometimes forgets,' said Eric, concealing his own apprehension.

Police had searched and made some enquiries while paying particular attention to places Richard had recommended. For the moment, they had given up. Richard said he would drive to some of the areas himself and continue looking, providing nothing else came to light.

There were two symphony concerts programmed for the next week. As a classical pianist and a soloist, Eric was an integral part of these concerts. He had to be there. Cynthia also had to go back to work. She was an administrator at the University of Tasmania and wanted desperately to re-engage. Besides, spending time with Imogen was gruelling.

'We need the money, Mum, we have to resume working,' said Eric.

'But what will I do here by myself?' she bewailed.

'What did you do when Dad was in Melbourne?'

'I went out to lunch with friends or had them over.'

'Why not have some friends here?'

'It's not the same, it's not the same,' she cried out.

Eric was losing patience with her. 'I feel for you, Mum. I know you miss Dad and this is an enormous adjustment. But why not just have one or two of your closest? Besides, the girls will be home from school about four-ish. I'll be about a bit. I need to practise here and at the concert hall, but I'll be around.'

Imogen did, in the long run, invite two of her best friends over for afternoon tea. It felt good, putting on one of her best outfits and makeup. Image was everything, she used to say. She never entertained the thought that their visit was far more about curiosity than sympathy.

Much was asked by her two friends. She told them Hughe had been under enormous pressure because of the important work he did for his clients. He became tired and depressed and took his own life as a result. They expressed their insincere pity. 'What a frightful thing to happen, Imogen. So sorry about this. And how are you feeling now?'

With kisses, hugs and goodbyes done, the two visitors were driving home and talking about Imogen's loss. Both concluded they didn't believe a word she uttered about Hughe's death. Something else was going on there, they presumed. Feeling secure in the privacy of the car, they released the façade of compassion. The women couldn't wait to be the first to tell the others of Imogen's demise and many gatherings were held in her absence. Gossip about her and Hughe was rife. She didn't know it yet, but Mrs Smyth, the ultimate socialite, had become an outcast.

The Smyth residence went up for sale. It was decided not to sell it by auction. An estate agent advised it would attract too many onlookers rather than genuine buyers. An American family purchased the property after the first inspection. It had only been listed for a day. The husband had been relocated and worked for the federal government as an attaché. He wasn't far from retirement and wanted to settle in Hobart when his service in Canberra came to an end. It suited him and his wife perfectly and they were prepared to pay more than the reserve to get it. If there was any positive to come out of this sale, Imogen thought, they were the perfect people to live in her house. It was a recompense of sorts and she felt vindicated for the effort she had put into her treasured home. One day she would visit them, introduce herself.

It took a day and into the early evening to move out the large quantity of possessions. Some items were bound for storage, some to Eric's house and that of friends. Other pieces of furniture were left in the house as part of the sale. A decision had to be made about the Steinway grand piano. It was too big for Eric's house and Imogen reluctantly agreed it wouldn't fit in a downsized dwelling. There was a long, drawn-out negotiation and heated argument. In the end, it was decided to loan it to the Hobart Symphony Orchestra. This was a benevolent gesture and at least Eric could continue to play it. Eric was well aware members of the orchestra would be dedicated to the care of this fine instrument.

It was one of Imogen's worst moments. The house, contents and grand piano were her life. She stayed in her room for a time. She wanted to die.

A single fronted house was found for Imogen, located near Sandy Bay, a ten-minute drive away from Eric's place. The process of finding her a home was torture for everyone involved. Rejection was her first reaction to any place presented to her. 'There's no room here, where will I put my things?' or, 'I don't like the kitchen, I don't like the paint on the walls, I don't like the street, what about a garden?' But the time arrived when she realised she had run out of objections. The whole process had become tiresome for her.

Recognition of changes to her life was painful to endure and was compounded when repeated phone calls and invitations to friends went unanswered. Nonetheless she kept up her appearance, including a new hairstyle and colour. Maintaining her sophisticated look was as important to her as breathing.

When a suitable time had passed, Imogen was invited to become a volunteer for the Red Cross. The Smyth's had a good reputation with this organisation due to their successful fundraising and they welcomed her with open arms. It was a start, she thought.

Gary was still to make contact with her. Sometimes, it kept her awake at night. She hoped one day she would hear from him, but doubts of a reunion crept more and more into her mind.

It was late in the day when Johnathan Lewis contacted Eric from the Melbourne office.

'I have some news, Eric, about Gary.'

'They've found him, thank God.'

'No, I'm sorry to say. I mentioned Gary to Margaret today. First time I've talked about him. She said he was here. He'd come for a quick visit and had lunch with your dad. Your father came back to the office at nine am the next morning to attend to a client and finalise some things. He seemed fine and said Gary told him he was going to take a flight early that morning for Alice Springs. That he was going out looking for another suitable location for his next group. Eric, I think you need to come to Melbourne. You need to see the police. They may be able to help,' said Johnathan.

'But what can they do? The police in the Northern Territory have already looked for him.'

'I understand that, but he was here, in Melbourne, they could do some investigations for you. I was coming back, but I'll stay here and wait for you. Can you come over tomorrow?' asked Johnathan.

'Okay, I'll come. But I don't know what they can do.' This was the last thing Eric wanted, but maybe Johnathan was right.

He told Cynthia about the latest news, packed and arrived in Melbourne, then caught a taxi to his late father's

Melbourne office. He realised he hadn't been there very often.

'Good afternoon, Margaret,' he said on entering the reception area.

'Oh, Mr Smyth. Good morning. It has been a long time since I last saw you. Please accept my condolences. Your father was a great man and well respected. It was an honour to work for him.'

'Thank you, Margaret, and thank you for the flowers you sent. You're very kind.'

On hearing his voice, Johnathan came out of the inner office. 'Hi, Eric, how was your flight?' he asked.

'Packed with scenarios.'

'I've taken the liberty of asking the police to come around. They'll be here in half an hour,' said Johnathan.

'Good, thanks, Johnathan.' Eric turned and smiled at Margaret before entering the inner office.

While waiting they both theorised on what may have happened. Forty-five minutes had passed before two police officers arrived and commenced a report about Gary's alleged disappearance.

'So, your brother was here for the day, then your father told Margaret, his assistant, that Gary had caught a plane back to Alice Springs. Is that correct?'

'Yes.'

'And your brother has not contacted any family member since?'

'No. As far as we knew he was back in Alice Springs. According to what my father relayed to Margaret; Gary was going to search for some out of the way camping destinations. This was usual practice for him. Contact from him could be sporadic, but he hasn't contacted our mother for a while or the guy who sometimes works with him – that is unusual. Apparently, the house is closed up and the Land Rover is still in the garage. That's even more unusual,' said Eric.

'Right. We'll go back to the station and make a few enquiries. The Northern Territory police haven't been able to locate him either?' asked the officer.

'No, nothing. Mind you, it's a huge area. Still, it is very troubling. His partner, Richard, said he was also going out to look for him.'

'We'll start an investigation. If we come up with anything we will let you know straight away. Hopefully we'll find out something today but no promises, of course.'

The officers left and Johnathan suggested they go out for a quick lunch.

'I can't fathom this. We've only just buried Dad and now Gary's gone missing. Christ.'

'They'll find him, Eric. He's out there unaware of just how much concern he's generated back here.'

They ate lunch in silence then slowly walked back to the office. Eric talked to Margaret for a time and Johnathan did paperwork. Late in the afternoon, police rang the office.

'Hello, Eric Smyth here.' He listened to the police at the other end then repeated it to Johnathan. 'The airlines are searching their records, it's still in progress, but at this stage, they don't think he caught a flight out. He may still be here in Melbourne. They will contact the Northern Territory police. I'll ring Richard now; I hope he's in range. Do you mind if I do that here in the office, Johnathan?'

'Not at all,' he replied.

'Fuck, fuck,' Eric said to himself.

Richard answered, he had just returned home. 'That might explain why we haven't been able to find him then, Eric. Any ideas of what's happened?'

'Not a clue. Thank you for what you've done, Ric. When and if we find out anything, I'll let you know.'

'No problem, Eric, I still think he'll turn up. Keep positive.'

Eric was talking with Johnathan. 'I'll have to go back home, give Mum the news. God knows how she's going to take it. She's just starting to get back on her feet. I can't do anything here. I'll give the police my contact details. If something surfaces, I'll come straight back.'

'How about we book a flight back together?' said Johnathan.

'That would be wonderful,' said Eric. 'Thank you.'

On the plane home Eric and Johnathan began to speculate again. Neither could give any logical reason for Gary's disappearance.

On his return, Eric explained the latest disclosures with his wife. They would both go and see Imogen.

An hour later Eric and Cynthia tried to keep calm as they sat in Imogen's crowded lounge room, while she went to make tea. She came back in, carrying her favourite tray and exquisite tea set. A set that was proudly brought out at every opportunity.

'You have something to tell me?' she asked while pouring tea and cutting up pieces of homemade cake.

'Mum … this is, this is … Mum, Gary is missing. He visited Dad in Melbourne; they had lunch and Gary was meant to catch a flight back the next morning. At this stage there is no record of him leaving Melbourne.'

She paused for a moment. 'Oh dear, I'd forgotten about that what with everything going on.'

'Mum! That was vitally important information, how could you forget it?'

'My husband died!' she said in a raised voice. 'Besides, I didn't think it had anything to do with him not ringing me.

How was I to know he was missing? Frankly, I think he's dead.'

'Oh Imogen, that's terrible. What makes you say that?' Cynthia asked.

'He never left it this long to contact me, never. Something is not right; I can feel it. Are you in constant contact with the police, Eric?'

'Of course, they will update me if they find out anything.'

After that, any talk was swallowed up. A long silence hung in the air while the three of them sat and thought.

One day, while practising piano for hours and finding himself on his own in the house, Eric decided to drive to Mount Nelson to give himself a break from the routine. He hoped it would smooth his screaming headache and constant, questioning mind.

On reaching the pinnacle he bought a coffee from the kiosk located at the summit. It had been erected to cater for the many visitors who came to this area for the stunning view of Hobart, the river and the history of the old signal station, which still stood in immaculate condition. Inside the station, visitors could read its interesting history.

It was a bright, cloudless day. There were only a few people about, which meant he could sit alone at the weathered, outdoor picnic table and ponder without intrusion. The Derwent River looked blue and calm. To his left was the city with its low office buildings. Nothing like the skyscrapers of Melbourne, but to him that was its charm. On his right were Sandy Bay and the Hobart Casino. On the other side of the river were other suburbs with numerous houses sprawled over the rolling hills. There was a clear view of the Tasman Bridge from here. He wondered how his father felt in those last moments before he jumped. Did he regret it immediately? Or was he glad to be deserting this world? Did he consider the sorrow this would bring to his family? *We'll never know*, thought Eric.

The past weeks had been psychologically draining and he was feeling wrung out. He wished his brother were here. It was a given that Gary was the stronger and more liberated of the two boys. Something Eric was never envious of. He preferred his literature and music, a complete contrast to Gary's obsession with the outdoors. They never regarded themselves close, but liked being in each other's company, regardless of those differing interests. He missed Gary's strength and presence more than ever. He admitted to himself his mother might be right and wondered how the family would cope with another disaster.

He let his mind wander, looking around his environment, taking in the spectacular view, feeling the warmth of the sun and remembering his wonderful wife and girls and Johnathan's unerring support. These thoughts began to fortify him, revive his dwindling spirit. In an hour he'd finished his second coffee and slowly walked to his car. Vivaldi's Four Seasons was playing at full volume as Eric slowly drove down the narrow winding road from Mount Nelson. He didn't want to get in touch with his mother today. He'd ring her tomorrow.

19. Melbourne

Mark was in the evidence room, looking in a box containing the few pieces of evidence found at Jacky Zhao's flat. He was asked by one the officers to come to the detective sergeant's office. While walking there he wondered why he was being summoned. He felt apprehensive.

The detective sergeant suggested Mark have a seat. Mark felt a few drops of sweat on his forehead.

'Sorry to have to tell you this, Mark, Zac was found in his flat. He'd been severely roughed up. Neighbours dialled for the police. They heard a commotion and some screaming. Whoever did it was gone by the time they arrived.'

'Jesus. I'm not surprised,' said Mark. 'I warned him this might happen. He was pretty sure of himself. Said he was safe.'

'You've been in contact with him?'

'Yeah. He rang a few nights ago. Wanted to apologise for threatening me with a gun, wanted us to remain friends, that sort of thing. We met at the Royal and had a couple of beers. I tried to get the name of his supplier. Said we could protect him. He wouldn't hear of it; said he'd never tell. It wasn't worth his life,' said Mark.

'Should have taken your advice. He's in hospital under police guard if you want to see him. He might talk to you now. He's in St Vincent's.'

Mark immediately drove to the hospital. In spite of the threat that Zac had made in pointing a gun at him and despite his sadness in the way Zac had ruined his life, Mark felt a need to help him. They had been friends for a long time, played footy together, went to nightclubs to drink and chat up the girls, shared each other's secrets and dreams. Zac had encouraged Mark to join the police force, something Mark was grateful for. He loved being a detective.

He showed his ID to reception and the officer stationed outside his ward. He hesitated a moment before entering, bracing himself for what he was about to see.

Zac was bruised over his face and arms. Both eyes were dark blue and swollen. He was taking some fluid through a straw and a drip was on a stand by his bed. He was severely injured and in pain.

'Hi, Zac, how are you going?'

Zac carefully moved his head to look at Mark. 'What do you fink?' He could barely open his mouth to talk.

'Do you know who did this?' Mark asked.

'Fucking fugs.' Zac's swollen lips prevented clear enunciation.

'Do you want to tell me now?' Mark asked.

'No, never.'

'We'll talk when you recover. Rest up and do what you're fucking told by the medics. You have a guard outside. I'll see you soon.' Mark left the room feeling sick to his stomach. He asked one of the nurses about Zac's condition.

'He's been hit over most of his body with a heavy object. He has significant bruising around his kidneys. He will recover over time.'

'Right, thanks.' He hurried back to the office and reported Zac's condition to his superior. The officers who first attended were writing up a report, so Mark went back to the evidence room. It didn't take long for him to locate what he was looking for. He signed it out, secured it in a plastic bag and zipped it up for safekeeping. He requested to have a look around Zac's house. Permission was granted. He took a couple of officers with him.

Donning blue gloves and footwear, they proceeded to look around the place. Most of the items inside the property were smashed or upturned, including Zac's prized tape player and a photo of him in his police uniform, smiling with a group of his colleagues.

'The whole place has been dusted, I assume?' Mark asked.

The officer confirmed it. 'At this stage I don't think they've found anything.'

Mark bent down and shone his torch on the handle of a cabinet. He'd noticed a strand of thick black hair stuck there. It would quiver faintly with any slight movement of air. Mark cautiously took it off the handle, pulled out a zip bag from his pocket and placed the hair inside. 'Probably Zac's, but better to check.' He handed it to the other officer.

Nothing else turned up so they left and went back to the station. The hair was registered and sent off to forensics. Being a pragmatist, he knew it might not conclusively reveal anything. *But you never know,* he thought.

20. Melbourne

Zac was well enough to come home from hospital. Mark decided he would help him as much as he could during his recuperation. Zac still carried some bruising, red patches and swelling to his face, but it was beginning to calm down.

'You sure you want to be here at your place?' asked Mark.

'Where else am I going to go?'

'Your parents, perhaps?'

'No way. For a start, they live in the country and, secondly, they are getting older and Dad's still not very well. I'm not going to hassle them with this. My sister said she would come down from Sydney for a few days. She'll stay with one of her friends and visit me every day. With both of you helping me, I'm going to be cared for.'

Julie had reluctantly cooked some food for Mark to take. Nonetheless, her vow to never forgive Zac for what he did to her husband remained. She was intransigent and would not change her view. Nor did she want Mark to become further involved. He did have some genuine reservations on what he was going to do but, ultimately, he had an ulterior motive – he convinced her it would become clearer.

Zac had the locks changed and installed another two locks for good measure. He also purchased some security cameras and alarms. He needed to replace his sound system but the TV still worked. He brought a new square dining table and a couple of chairs. They came in a flat-pack, so he busied himself putting it together. He had a little money put in the bank although it was imperative he find work straightaway. Most of the bruises were gone so he could start enquiring.

'You're not afraid they'll return?' asked Mark. He had come to see Zac with a couple of beers.

'Nope, they wanted to teach me a lesson. They'd be satisfied now.' He suddenly got up to go to the toilet. 'I've got the bloody runs. Give me a minute.'

Mark took his chance and darted to the bedroom. He pulled an item from his pocket and compared it to something hanging on the clothes rack.

By the time Zac came back from the toilet, Mark was calmly drinking from his bottle of beer and they resumed their discussion.

'Better?' asked Mark.

'It's the medication that's helping me keep off the drugs, I think, or this particular beer of yours,' he said with a grin. On Monday Mark was in the detective superintendent's office with two other officers. They were strategising behind closed doors.

'Wire me up. I think he's ready to talk,' said Mark.

'We'll do that, of course, but this has to be planned first, as you know,' said one of the officers.

'Let's frame a plan together and be ready to go in a week. I'll keep in contact so I can be sure of his movements,' said Mark. The officers agreed.

Mr Li had been to the station on three occasions asking for Jacky Zhao's body. With the help of the interpreter, Mark was able to placate him, but only just. Relatives in China were demanding Jacky's release.

'How is he?' Li asked during his visit.

'What do you mean?' Mark was puzzled at the query.

'How is he? How is he?' Li kept repeating his question, becoming impatient with Mark and stabbing his index finger in the air to emphasise. 'How is he?' he said again. This time accompanied by a forced smile revealing stained teeth.

'I have no idea who you mean,' said Mark, completely bewildered.

Mr Li gave up and started walking away, mumbling to himself. Mark watched him leave and noticed his diminutive statue and somewhat bowed legs. *What a strange guy,* he thought.

21. Hobart

There was still limited information regarding Gary's disappearance. A protracted search by the airlines confirmed they couldn't locate the name Gary Smyth travelling to Alice Springs. They did find his name entering Melbourne. Victoria Police had issued notices to the media and in print. The item was accompanied by the latest photo of Gary, which had been taken a few years earlier. Eric had offered it, hoping it would stir someone's memory. One person reported they might have seen him leaving Chinatown late in the day. But they weren't sure. There were always lots of people around that time of day. And a member of staff at the restaurant thought they remembered him, but they weren't entirely sure either. The hotel, where Gary had been staying, reported a compact backpack had been left in his room. They had tried to make contact via his mobile but their messages were never returned. They were in the process of sending it back to his Alice Springs address. Police contacted Eric to say they would like to pick it up and search it. It may provide some clues.

Back at the station police went through Gary's bag thoroughly. There was nothing out of the ordinary within its folds or pockets, just a few personal items that had been packed for an overnight stay. Cleaners had been to the room and other guests had since stayed. It had been booked out three times over since Gary had stayed there. Investigating the room would be a waste of time.

Eric said he would come over and pick the bag up. There was nothing else the police could do with it.

His mother was informed about the latest but remained unmoved. She was convinced he was dead.

'You haven't cried about him, Mum,' said Eric.

'I can't cry anymore. I just want him home so we can say our goodbyes and put him next to his father. Something awful must have happened. He wouldn't leave without his things, not catch his flight. No, something has gone wrong. I know it. I still believe he's dead.'

Imogen began to lose interest in volunteering for the Red Cross and they were at a loss about where to put her. She didn't want to help assemble first aid kits, volunteer in a Red Cross shop or help with answering the numerous phone enquiries. She was unused to wearing anything but her expensive clothing. Putting on any apparel emblazoned with the Red Cross logo was out of the question for her and not negotiable. In the end, she refused her help and left.

'What are you going to do now, Mum? You can't just sit here every day rolling around in self-pity. You have to find something to do.'

The family were at their wits end.

'I want my old life back,' Imogen stated emphatically. She still remained frustrated about her dwindling position in the community. The slow realisation of falling to the lower rung of the society ladder was agonising.

'You have to face it, Mum, that part of your life is over.'

This brought her to tears. Eric understood it was heartless, pointing out the obvious, but he was becoming weary of trying to lift her moods. She had to help herself out of it.

'Right now, I'm more panicked about Gary's whereabouts. You may be right, I don't know, we don't know. I'm going to Melbourne tomorrow to pick up his backpack. I'd like you to have a good think about your next move. There must be something out there you would like to immerse yourself in. Your talents can be put to good use. If you have to wear an apron or something, who cares?'

She nodded, bowed head and blew her nose. 'I'll have a good think about it.'

He left her, sitting in her favourite lounge chair, head down, wiping her nose with a lace handkerchief. Driving home he thought perhaps he had been too unfair on her then dismissed it. Finding Gary was far more important than pandering to his mother's unrealistic needs.

22. Melbourne

Eric arrived in Melbourne and went directly to the police station. He had a long meeting with the police officers where they advised him of investigations and interviews that had been completed so far.

'We haven't found out much at the moment, this is still ongoing,' said one of the officers. 'Rest assured we will do whatever we can to find your brother. Is there any reason you can think of that would entice him to want to disappear?'

'Absolutely none. He was happy with his life. Loved the outdoors and taking people on camping trips to some remote outback places. He was in his element. He loved what he did,' said Eric.

'Do you know if he had any enemies? Did he take drugs or owe money?'

'No, never. He hated drugs. He was a health fanatic and if he ever wanted money, he knew he could always ask Dad. There was never any hint of money struggles or debt,' said Eric.

'Excuse me for asking, but your father recently committed suicide, is that correct?' asked the officer.

'How did you know that?' Eric became defensive about this line of questioning.

'We have to look into other possibilities if we are to solve this.'

'This was purely coincidental. One has nothing to do with the other. The family are as in the dark about this as you are. Unless you know something we don't?'

'No, we don't, but we had to be sure. Are you staying long?'

'No, I'm catching a flight back today,' said Eric.

'We know how anxious you must be. We'll keep looking into it.'

He thanked those who were working on his brother's disappearance and walked to a nearby café. Sitting at an outside table drinking coffee, he watched the throng of people walking past. Some were moving hurriedly, intent on their destination, some more slowly while laughing and talking, and some were holding the hands of their children who were skipping, excited at being in the city. He held Gary's backpack close to his chest as if it would make his brother appear. He wished he would emerge from the crowd, alive, walk towards him with his bright smile and tanned face. A few tears started to well up in the corner of his eyes. *Wishing is not helping*, he thought.

On the plane traveling to Hobart, he was tempted to open the backpack, but decided against it. Better to wait when he could look through it thoroughly at home. At times the plane hit some turbulence that woke him from a light sleep. He shot a furtive glance at some of the passengers and wondered if any of them had suffered a family tragedy. Did anyone notice his troubled, pale, tired face? *You're being ridiculous, of course they don't. God help me, I think I'm going mad.*

23. Melbourne

It was early Thursday when Mark and the team decided they were prepared and ready to go. A warrant had been issued; Mark was wired to record anything Zac might reveal. An unmarked police car would be stationed outside with two officers ready to assist.

It was confirmed Zac would be home. He had recovered well. Bruises had almost disappeared and a check-up gave him the all clear, although his kidneys were still tender. His application as a bouncer had been accepted and he was to start in the next fortnight. It was quite a comedown from being a highly respected detective, but he hadn't given up the notion of being accepted back. He felt he deserved a second chance.

Mark was in two minds. On the one hand, he felt a modicum of guilt about the entrapment, but, overwhelmingly, he felt entirely justified. Zac had to face what he had done. He had to be charged and jailed. That was the law and Mark didn't make any exceptions.

Zac welcomed him; he was more than ready to have a beer and a yarn with his friend Mark.

'Come in, come in. How have you been?' asked Zac.

'It's been pretty busy. Wow, you look so much better. Bruising just about gone. How's the rest of you?'

'I'm feeling great and, in case you're wondering, I'm completely clean. Haven't touched the stuff or ever will again,' said Zac.

Mark sat while Zac prepared snacks. He came back with two large bowls filled to the brim with potato chips and salted cashews.

'What's happening at the station?'

'You know I can't talk about that, Zac.'

'Of course, of course. Old habits.' He was slightly embarrassed at his assumptions. 'How's Julie then?'

'She's good, working, trying to solve the insolvable as usual.'

The two men drank, ate and talked. Zac was happy and relaxed and spoke about his upcoming job and plans for his future.

'I think if I can prove I'm a changed man, the force might accept me back.'

'Zac, that's not going to happen. You stole your gun, you were on drugs while on the job, you stole an amount of heroin. What did you expect would happen? How could you let it get so out of control?'

'Don't lecture me again, Mark, I know what I've done.'

'Do you, Zac? Do you? Is there anything else you want to tell me?'

'If you're trying to find out the identity of my supplier, you've got no chance. You saw what they did to me; I'm lucky to be alive. If they have an inkling I've given you a name, I'm dead.'

Mark was silent while looking straight into Zac's eyes. He pulled a plastic bag from his side pocket. 'Do you recognise this, Zac?'

'Yeah, it's a couple of buttons. So?' Zac avoided eye contact.

'These buttons were found on the floor of Jacky Zhao's flat. Do you know why they were there?'

'No. What the fuck are you getting at?' Zac gave an awkward laugh.

'They are from the sleeve of your jacket, Zac. I know because I've matched it.'

'Pfft. Are you bloody joking? That could belong to anyone, or any jacket.'

'That jacket is part of a suit that was tailor-made for you, Zac. You had it made for our wedding. It's unique,' said Mark.

'You're fucking kidding me.' Zac leapt from his chair, knocking the table over. Half empty beer bottles smashed to the floor; the contents flowed towards the kitchen cupboards. Chips and nuts became part of the liquid and made the floor slippery and uneven. He momentarily slipped but regained his balance. As he opened the front door, Mark grabbed him. Zac swung a punch that landed near Mark's eye. Mark returned with a sudden punch to Zac's stomach. They both fell to the floor and were rolling around in the slimy mess, each trying to overcome the other. Zac located Mark's gun, pulled it out of the holster, got up to his knees and pointed it straight at him.

Mark raised his hands, shielding his face. 'Don't do it, Zac, don't do it. You'll never get away with it. There's a better way out of this.' He was sure he was going to be shot. He knew in a split second he could be dead. He tried to not show his fear. Mark kept talking in the hope it would distract Zac from firing the gun.

Zac stood up while keeping his aim steady. He slipped again and the bullet he fired caught the top of Mark's ear.

Hearing the shot, the police back-up sprinted up the stairs while at the same time sending a message for more help. Zac was darting from the door; he was immediately overpowered. The uniforms whipped the gun from his hand, forcibly stood him upright and pulled his hands around to his back.

Mark managed to get up to his feet; he was short of breath. He directed the officers to handcuff Zac's wrists.

'Zac Harris, I am arresting you on suspicion of the murder of Jacky Zhao. You don't have to say or do anything, but if you do, it may be used in evidence against you.'

'You set me up. You fucking bastard, you set me up!' Zac was furious.

A doctor stitched up Mark's ear and gave him antibiotics. 'Just keep an eye on it and come and see me in a week. You're a very lucky man, that was close,' he said.

'Tell me about it.' Mark was still on edge.

Back at the station Mark was writing up a report. His left eye was swollen and painful, requiring him to periodically apply an ice pack. His ear was numb. He'd cleaned himself the best he could and was looking forward to a shower at home. Cleanse himself of the day, body and soul. His suit was a mess and would have to be dry-cleaned. But he didn't care. Zac was in custody and he was thankful. It went to plan. He had a meeting with his superior who praised him for his work.

'Finish this up tomorrow, go home. You need a couple of days rest.'

'I'll finish my report first and I need to go back to the premises to do a search. Thank you, sir.'

They shook hands.

Mark and an officer went back to Zac's place. He hoped to find something but the search could be futile. Worth a try, nonetheless. Just as they were about to give up, he noticed a cupboard standing against the back wall of a spare room. Most of it was concealed by various sports equipment and other odds and ends. *Maybe they didn't think it was important during the initial search,* he thought. Mark had to pull apart all the high and roughly stacked items before he could reach the steel double doors. It didn't have a lock. With the two doors wide open, he felt through the pockets of a couple of hoodies. Nothing. There was one high shelf at the back. He stood on his toes and pulled out two ski jackets, gloves and a pair of ski boots. He stretched his arm further to reach the back and located a container. He opened it, then put it in his safest pocket.

Before leaving, they made a few enquiries of other residents in the complex. One was able to provide Mark with Zac's movements and was willing to sign a witness statement.

Back at the station Mark completed his report, signed in the container as evidence then drove home. He felt completely fatigued. When he pulled up, Julie came out to greet him.

'Mark, what's happened to you? Your clothes are covered in something.' Then she noticed his injuries. 'Oh my God, Mark, look at you, you've been hit. Your eye is terribly swollen. Why didn't you contact me to bring you home?' She tried not to reveal her panic. 'What's wrong with your ear?'

'I'm okay, darling, I'm okay. Let's get inside.'

Mark took a long shower, then he and Julie sat together each sipping a glass of wine while he revealed the entire dismal story.

'He tried to shoot you again, Mark. I hope you now realise he is a different person, he's no longer the friend and colleague you once knew. I feel so bad about your loss, but I love you, you are all I care about. Please don't ever, ever trust in him again.'

'You can count on that.' Silence, then, 'Forget that self-deprecating stuff, he was a dynamic guy, he just never realised it. And he was a brilliant detective. Drugs are a bloody curse. He's completely lost his way. He's become delusional too, thinks if he behaves and is clean of drugs the force would take him back.' Mark looked up to the ceiling; his eyes were moist with tears he grittily held back from falling down his face. He'd finally accepted the Zac he had known was no more. Julie held him for a long time.

24. Hobart

The plane landed on time; Cynthia was at the airport to pick Eric up.

'Have you looked inside the back pack?' she asked.

'Not yet. I don't expect its contents will reveal anything. The police have searched through it.'

'Are they still examining the case?'

'Yes, they said they will do what they can to find him. I think Mum's right though. I'm beginning to believe he's not alive.'

'I'm so sorry, Eric. Not knowing is cruel.'

They sat down for dinner. When the girls went to bed, Eric put the backpack on the table and unzipped it. There wasn't much to see. It contained the usual items of someone who was only staying for one night. Eric put his hands over the now empty pack, hoping there would be some clue hidden in the lining.

'There's nothing in there, love.' Cynthia put her arm around his shoulder and drew him to her. The sadness he had held back now spilled out. In the space of a few weeks, he had lost his father and now his brother was missing.

Next morning, he visited Imogen. She hadn't found

anything else of interest to volunteer for. She reasoned her considerable contribution and talents were ignored. The loss of her husband and disappearance of her son were not enough to let her have her own way either. She was in a black mood. 'I told you. Knew you wouldn't find anything else,' she scolded him.

'Hey, don't speak to me like that. I needed to bring his belongings back. What did you expect? They would send it in the post?'

'I'm hurting.'

'I know that! You must recognise that you are not the only one hurting here. I have a profession that needs practise, attendance and concentration. I am handling Dad's and your affairs. I have a family I need to spend time with while feeling absolutely distraught about what has happened. And what exactly do you do? You whinge – you whinge because you're no longer the queen of Hobart. You can't show off your exclusive clothing and jewellery, take jealous little socialites around your spacious house while deliberately pointing out its expensive contents. You're a narcissist, did you know that? You can't survive without constant attention. How much do you think that craving for attention cost Dad? Have you thought about that? Has your selfish little mind ever entered the world of reality and worked out just how hard he tried to make you happy? You're not upset about the loss of Dad. You're upset about the loss of attention.'

'How dare you.' Imogen was incensed. She sprung from her chair and slapped Eric across the face.

He grabbed her hand. 'Don't ever do that to me again. Gary and I suffered a lot from your frightening temper. He escaped you, but I'm still here. One more act like that and I, and my family, will abandon you, just like everyone else has done. Now, try and find some humility, if you can, and look for something to make yourself useful and helpful to the community.' He strode out and went to see Johnathan.

It was another late afternoon meeting and Eric was sitting talking to Mick while waiting. He could hear a forceful phone call taking place in the inner office.

'Any word?' asked Mick.

'No, unfortunately. It's the not knowing. Whatever the outcome, we need to know even if it's the worst. It's eating away at us.'

'Yes, yes, understand,' said Mick.

Eric needed to change the subject. 'And what about you? Any girlfriend yet?' He asked Mick with a look of interest.

'No, no.' Mick was going red with embarrassment. 'It's not like that.'

'What do you mean?'

'Oh nothing, nothing. It's been pretty busy here,' he said, wanting to stop where this chat was going.

'Come on, what do you mean? It's not like that?' He suspected Mick was gay. A couple in the orchestra were and Eric had, some time ago, come to realise it. Homosexuality had been decriminalised in Tasmania. Being a compassionate, perceptive man, he espoused the right of two people to love each other, irrespective of their sexual preferences. He wanted Mick to know he liked and respected him. Eric was appreciative of the good work he did for Hughe. His professionalism and attention to detail were often mentioned by Eric's father.

'Dad often said you were his right-hand man, Mick.'

'Oh, did he? Thank you, Eric, I—' He was interrupted. Johnathan came out of the inner office.

'Sorry to keep you, Eric, a trying client,' he said raising his eyes to the ceiling. 'Come in, come in. Would you like a drink, alcoholic substance perhaps? You look drained, if I may say so.'

'Yes, to both of those, thank you.'

'Mick, a couple of glasses please and bring one for yourself. I think we could use a drink today.'

Johnathan poured three beers and Mick took his back to his desk. 'He works above and beyond that lad. Couldn't do without him. So, bring me up to speed.'

'There's nothing much to tell. I told you about the backpack, didn't I?' Eric was trying to remember; so much was happening, forgetting things had become more common.

'Yes, you did. Anything?'

'No, nothing. Just a bag full of overnight stuff. I felt around the lining too.' He gave a quiet moan. 'I had a row with Mother today – she slapped my face. Not for the first time, I might add. Gary and I suffered her bad moods on many occasions.'

'I'm very sorry to hear that, Eric. Can't say I'm surprised. I always had the impression she was a tight coil ready to spring open with a vengeance. Your dad was sometimes the recipient of her tendency to lash out. He confided it to me once or twice. He loved her though, you see, wanted to do the very best for her.'

'I don't get that kind of marriage. There is a limit to forgiveness. I can't tell you how riled I am with her since Dad died,' said Eric.

'Your anger is reasonable under the circumstances. Don't reproach yourself too much.'

They had another couple of drinks and talked more about Gary's disappearance, each proffering their own speculations.

'Frankly, I'm beginning to come around to mother's assertion. If she's right, I'm very baffled about how. That keeps me awake at night.'

'Keep hoping and keep an open mind, Eric. He may just call you out of the blue and be dumbfounded why you were so worried about him.'

'You could be right, you could be right,' said Eric.

When he left, Johnathan opened another beer and thought for a while. He didn't want to say it, but he agreed with Imogen. Looking at the options logically, he also suspected Gary was dead.

25. Melbourne

The formal interrogation of Zac was about to commence. Two detectives from the crime squad were in the sparse room with him. Another officer was preparing the video to record the interview. Zac was sitting upright on one of the wooden chairs, his hands clasped and resting on the desk. His lawyer sat alongside him, a law pad open, ready for notes. The detectives sat opposite. Mark watched from behind the one-way glass.

'It is nine-thirty am and Detective Olsen and Detective Ferguson are conducting this interview. For the record, can you state your full name, address and date of birth, please,' said Detective Olsen.

'Zac Nathan Harris. Unit 1, 20 Auburn Street, South Yarra. 10 June 1962.'

'You understand why you are here today?' said Detective Olsen.

'Yes. I've been accused of having something to do with the death of Jacky Zhao, based on the very flimsy evidence of a self-righteous former colleague.'

Zac's lawyer whispered to him.

'Can you tell us where you were on the night of 15 April this year?' asked Detective Olsen.

'I was tired in the wake of a long day working on an investigation. I had something to eat and had an early night,' said Zac.

'We have a witness statement stating your car was seen leaving your premises at nine pm on the night of the fifteenth, returning at approximately ten-fifteen pm then leaving again approximately thirty minutes later. Is that correct?'

'They're mistaken,' said Zac.

Detective Olsen put a container on the table, opened it and took out a bullet. Zac's neck turned red; he looked stunned.

'This bullet was fired from the police-issue handgun you took with you when you disappeared and have since handed in. Can you explain that, Zac?'

Zac turned to his lawyer; they whispered to each other.

'No comment,' said Zac.

Detective Ferguson handed a plastic bag to Detective Olsen. He held it up for Zac to see.

'These two buttons, which were found in Jacky Zhao's premises, are an exact match to the missing buttons from your jacket. The jacket is part of a suit tailor-made for you, Zac. Can you tell us about that?'

'No comment,' said Zac. His voice became subdued, his head bent lower but his eyes remained fixed on the officer. The confident Zac of a few minutes ago had started to wane.

'A week ago, Detective Mark Amos visited you. During that visit he showed and asked you about this particular piece of evidence. You punched Detective Amos, attempted to run, fought with him then pointed and fired a gun at him. Could you talk to us about that day, Zac?'

'No comment. I want a moment with my lawyer.'

The officers left the room and joined Mark who was still watching them.

'He's guilty all right,' said Detective Ferguson.

A few minutes went by, then the lawyer opened the door and they entered the room. The detectives remained standing.

'Zac Nathan Harris, we are charging you with the suspected murder of Jacky Zhao. You do not have to say anything. Anything you do or say may be given as evidence in court proceedings against you,' said Detective Olsen.

Zac didn't say anything. He put his hands behind his back and hung his head. He was remanded in custody.

Mark no longer felt any compassion for his former friend. He was, however, flummoxed. Why? Why on earth would he kill Jacky Zhao?

26. Hobart

Eric hadn't spoken to his mother since their last meeting. One day she turned up without prior notice.

'Come in,' Cynthia spoke politely, but expressed no affection toward Imogen. Like everybody else, she had become tired of indulging her.

'Is Eric in?' asked Imogen.

'Yes, he's at the piano reading music. There's a concert on Saturday.'

'I see. Could you ask him if he will see me, please?'

'No, Imogen, you can ask him yourself. Your mother is here, Eric,' Cynthia said, loud enough for him to hear.

Eric appeared. 'What do you want?' he said bluntly.

'I'm not here to apologise but …'

'Then get out.'

'What did you say?'

'You heard, Mother, I said get out.'

For a moment no one spoke.

'If I say sorry, can I stay?' she asked.

'Only if you mean it.'

'Yes, all right, all right, I'm sorry, I am. I shouldn't have hit you, Eric, that was inexcusable. My whole life has changed, just like that. Changing habits at this time of life is a big ask.'

'You have always been a volatile person, Mum. Hitting your children was the norm. Never do that again.' Eric turned to go back to his piano; he was not going to let his mother off lightly.

'I promise I won't. And you were right. I need to do something for the community. I've just started in the kitchen of the Salvation Army; they feed a lot of poor people. And I'm wearing an apron.'

'Pleased to hear that, Mum.' He still refrained from embracing her. A lot of history came to the fore when she slapped his face. He wasn't ready to pardon her. 'I think now is the right time to show you something.' Eric left the room, re-entering with an envelope. 'I'm expecting you will be upset about this, but you need to see it. I kept it from you because, at the time, you were in no state to read this letter. It's for you.'

Imogen opened the letter and slowly read the words Hughe had lovingly written to his wife. Then she read it again. The tears Eric was expecting to see didn't materialise.

'This makes me so livid, so, so livid. How dare he. He blames me; he has the audacity to blame me. He says it wasn't my fault then says he did it all to make me happy. I didn't ask him to steal from druggies, put his family in danger or us in debt. I never ever asked him to do any of that. Why didn't he tell me he couldn't afford it? Then he takes the coward's way out, commits suicide, abandons his family, leaving us to deal with his chaos. Now I know why you asked if I knew how much my craving for attention cost your father. No, I didn't know, I had no idea. Sure, I like attention, who doesn't? But I refuse to make allowances for what he did. I hate him for this. He's wrecked my life.' She angrily threw the letter at Eric, picked up her things and walked out, leaving the front door wide open.

Eric and Cynthia sat in their lounge room, speechless.

The girls had woken up during Imogen's outburst, witnessing her livid temper and enraged exit from the house. The parents reassured them, said they were not to worry: 'Grandma was a bit shaken up about a letter. It's okay now.' They shrugged, went back to their room, not totally believing the explanation but they had exams coming up. A good night's sleep was needed.

'I didn't expect that reaction,' said Cynthia.

'Nor me. It further proves just how unwilling she it to take responsibility for anything. She's selfish. She will always be selfish. I don't want to see her for a while, Cynthia. If she calls, don't answer; if she comes here, don't open the door. My family don't need to be repeatedly exposed to her instability and rage. Enough is enough. I want to focus my attention on Gary's disappearance.'

'And I support you,' she said.

27. Melbourne

Zac was now in remand. Mark felt enough time had passed to attempt a visit. He didn't know if Zac would see him or open up if he did, but he had to try.

He went through security checks then he sat and waited. Fifteen minutes went by then Zac appeared and sat opposite.

'Thanks for seeing me,' said Mark.

'I sat on it for a while. You're the reason I'm here; you set me up,' said Zac. His tone was belligerent.

'Zac, you are the reason for being here and you would have done the same thing if you suspected me of breaking the law. Don't forget, you tried to kill me – twice.'

'What do you want?'

'I'll get straight to the point. Why did you kill Jacky? It doesn't make any sense.'

'If you knew the whole story, it makes sense,' said Zac.

'Tell me the whole story then.'

Zac laughed. 'Are you joking? I'd be a dead man. I told you before, no way.' He got up to leave.

'What if we could protect you? Put you in protective custody?'

'And what's in it for me?' Zac asked.

'Get the bastards at the top. The ones who got you into this predicament in the first place.'

'Tell you what, I'll think about it. Come back next week. We'll talk further.' Zac walked to the door then turned around. 'I do take what I've done seriously and I miss you, my friend. Just want you to know that.' The door buzzed and he went through.

At least he's talking to me, thought Mark. *That's a start.*

Mark and Julie had some friends over for dinner and gin rummy. There was a lot of gaiety around the table as well as some serious competition. It was a fun, relaxed night for everyone, especially Mark. Their friends left in the early hours and Mark was lying in bed watching Julie undress.

'Has anyone told you how stunning you are?' he asked, looking at her with admiration.

'Not the way you do.'

She climbed into bed beside him. They had loving, passionate sex. Mark's apprehensions were swept from his mind. He slept peacefully for the first time in weeks.

It was Saturday morning. Mark was outside with his coffee, walking around on the concrete pavers admiring their well-tended rear garden. The sun was up and he felt happy. Julie brought out his mobile. 'It's the detective sergeant.'

He put the phone to his chest so nothing could be heard. 'Damn,' he said, wistfully looking at his wife. He was hoping for a relaxed day with her. He took a deep breath. 'Mark Amos.' He listened to the detective sergeant. 'I see, right, thanks for letting me know.' He put the phone down on the outside table, turned to the kitchen window and looked at Julie.

She knew that look and went straight to him. 'What's wrong?'

'Zac has committed suicide.'

'What! How?'

'Overdose.'

'But how did he get hold of the stuff to do that?' Julie was incredulous.

'There'll be an investigation, naturally, but we may never know. Sometimes drugs get into the system. They're undeterred by our up-to-date security. He's been off drugs for ages. Oh … fuck it! He didn't have to do this. He's left a note for me apparently. I'll have to go into the station, sorry, darling. Listen, don't say anything to Dad or Rebecca or anyone.'

'No, I would never do that, I know the rules,' Julie said.

'I know you do; just thought I would remind you. I'll be back when I can.' Mark kissed her and left.

A briefing was taking place when he arrived at the station. Attending was the detective sergeant, detective senior sergeant, two officers from the drug squad, himself and another detective from the homicide squad. There were some notes written on a whiteboard. Mark quietly sat down and listened.

Zac was now at the morgue and one of the officers was asking if anything was known about how the drugs came into his possession.

'We don't know at this stage. The initial response from one of the prison officers at the remand centre suspects it may be heroin. A search of prisoners in remand is being prepared at the moment. They are not confident of finding anything, but we'll see.'

Most at the briefing started to leave. Mark stayed behind to speak to his superior.

'How are you feeling, Mark?' he asked.

'I'm fine, thanks. I keep thinking what a waste. I thought that before he was remanded. I believe he left me a note?'

'Yes, I have it here. If there is anything in the note that would assist us, we need to know. Please pass it back to me,' said the detective sergeant.

'Of course. I'll read it here and give it straight back.'

With some trepidation Mark sat at his desk and unfolded the crumpled, smudged page. The paper was lined, tattered and torn on one side, with the words written in pencil. Some words had lines scratched across them, indicating Zac was struggling to find a way of describing his thoughts.

Well, this is it then – the end of it – what a balls up – I have fucked up big time – no point saying I'm sorry – what good ~~wit~~ would that do – I hope you get to read this Mark – you were my best friend and I hurt you, I know that, but then the bloody drugs became my best friend – I don't know why I let it come to this – you'll want to know my supplier – it's Mr Li who owns the restaurant – such a sly bastard, it was one of his thugs who bashed me up – I was never able to find out where he gets the drugs from, I hope you do. I ~~mur~~ killed Jacky because I suspected he spotted me as the man arguing with Li at the back of the restaurant one day. I couldn't pay for drugs at the time and Li was not at all pleased – Jacky witnessed it – when I went to his flat, he strongly denied remembering me – but I shot ~~at~~ him just the same because I didn't believe him – I cleaned up – forgot to properly get rid of the bullet, wish I had. Shows you how out of my mind I was. Drugs numb your feelings – you're not human – now that I'm off 'em, I feel so much pain – I can't deal with what I did – who I've become.
Goodbye my friend
Zac

When he'd finished reading, Mark began to rock slowly back and forth in his chair, ending with his elbows on the desk, head in his hands. He was shaken. *What a waste, what a fucking waste, those fucking scum, selling this stuff, ruining lives,* he thought. He pulled himself together and returned the note to his superior. He informed him of its contents and requested a warrant to search Li's premises, then went home to Julie.

Having checked opening hours, the police officers entered Li's restaurant early in the morning and issued him with a copy of the warrant to search his residence. They bundled him into the police car and drove him to his house where the drug squad were waiting, along with an interpreter.

'I no understand, why you take me? I do nothing wrong,' he kept repeating over and over again. The officers remained silent.

On reaching his place, they took him inside and the interpreter explained in Mandarin what was happening.

'I no have drugs, I no have drugs,' he kept protesting, louder and louder.

It didn't take long to find them. The drugs were stashed in suitcases hidden in the attic. A thorough search didn't find a notebook with a list of names, which was disappointing, but they had taken some drugs off the streets at least.

The officers read him his rights, handcuffed him and took him back to the station.

Li was sitting in a corner of the interview room with the interpreter next to him. Two detectives were sitting at a table. The interview was being recorded and Mark stood behind the one-way glass. Li's rights, date of birth, address and other information had been recorded.

'Now, Mr Li, we want you to tell us where you buy the drugs we found in your house today,' said the detective.

'They not mine, I not buy them, someone put them in house,' said Li, who was clearly frightened.

'It would be better for you to cooperate and tell us where you obtain the drugs, Mr Li.'

The interpreter was helping translate.

'You have never been in trouble before, Mr Li. You run a very good restaurant. You wanted to give your nephew a chance of a good life in Australia. Why then are you dealing in drugs? asked the detective.

This time, Li spoke without the interpreter. 'They make me. They kill me if I tell you name.'

'What? Someone made you sell drugs. Who made you? Tell us. We can protect you.'

Li and the interpreter talked for five minutes. She then passed on the details. 'He drives to New South Wales then sits in his car at the wharf until it gets dark. One of the fishing boats has the drugs on board. He loads some drugs into two suitcases, pays in cash, puts the suitcases in the boot then drives back to Melbourne. Depending on demand, he does the trip maybe every one or two months; he has never been picked up,' said the interpreter.

'Where is the wharf?' asked the detective.

More talk ensued between Mr Li and his interpreter. 'He can show you on a map,' she said.

A map was brought in and Li bent over it in deep concentration, his bent finger slowly tracing the east coast, then he found it and pointed to a wharf where he met his contact.

'What is the name of the boat?' asked the detective.

'I not know name, is little boat.'

'What is the name of the man on the boat?'

'I not know name of man on boat. I take parcel from him and put in car. I pay him with money. I go.'

Another hour was spent questioning Mr Li. During the interrogation, they were able to gain a description and position of where the boat usually moored. New South Wales Police were notified.

'How did you find out about the boat and the drugs?'

The question caused a longer conversation between Li and the interpreter.

'He tells me he had a friend who told him the drugs come in one boat then another boat to Australia.'

'What is the name of the friend? We would like to talk with him,' asked the drug squad officer.

She asked him. 'He says he is dead and that is why he is frightened because they will kill him too.'

Li was charged with possession and sent to jail awaiting trial. The restaurant had to be closed. Staff were disgruntled and disappointed they had lost their jobs, and had not been paid for the last two weeks. Rumours were rampant about their former boss. Maybe he killed the man in the lane. Suspicion about Li abounded amongst the staff for days. They hoped one day the restaurant would open again, but for now it was lifeless.

Later, Li would plead guilty and would be sent to jail for four years. He was kept away from other prisoners for his safety. His interpreter visited him sometimes and furnished him with newspapers from China, which he read eagerly and with gratitude. As a consequence of his exemplary conduct, and the confidence of correction officers that he was no longer at risk, he was permitted to work in the prison kitchen where he demonstrated his cooking skills. Officers found him to be so happy they thought he would never want to leave. Jacky Zhao's body was released and repatriated back to China.

28. Melbourne

Zac's suicide and his note had a profound effect on Mark. And Zac's family were deeply hurt and grief-stricken over his death. Their loss, incalculable. Mark tried to comfort them. He told them about Zac's achievements as a competent, intelligent detective. But his words seemed deficient under the circumstances. He felt helpless.

Zac's body was flown back to New South Wales for a service and burial. Mark was too devastated to attend; instead, he took a week off. His sleep was intermittent and he sometimes paced around the house, coffee in hand, thinking. He felt he had failed his former friend and his death depressed him. He weighed the possibility of leaving the force.

'You love the work, Mark. I think you would regret it. It's what you do best. Give it time,' Julie said.

She was right, he did go back, sat at his familiar desk and leafed through some of the files. There was no doubt he was meant to do this work. This is where he belonged.

The body found in the lane was still in the morgue. The pathologist hadn't been able to provide anything new. He left it until last then opened that file again. *Maybe we missed something*, he thought. Just then his superior asked him into the office.

'Good to have you back,' he said. 'I want to show you some footage from the prison where Li is. Have a look at this. Now, this guy wasn't on the list Li declared as people he would like to visit him. There was only a couple and they were approved. One of those names was his solicitor. This guy in the footage presented a card from a solicitor's office. Said Mr Li had forgotten to tell them. Li was asked if he wanted to see the solicitor and, of course, he said yes. So, there is this guy sitting, waiting and in walks Li to see him. Watch the body language and his face. Look at the way Li gradually sits down. He's frightened, I'm in no doubt. They exchange a few words then Li gets up and requests to go back to his cell. The guy walks out. Do you recognise him?'

'No, unfortunately. Do we know his name or anything about him?'

'We know he's not a solicitor. Li is tight-lipped; claims he has never seen him before. "I not know him; I not see him before." You know, the usual denial,' said the detective sergeant.

'Do we have any photos on file of him?' said Mark.

'Have a look if you like, but where do you start?'

'Good question.'

Time was flying. Mark noticed it was already four o'clock. He'd just come back from a homicide incident. A woman was found dead on the nature strip with a dead man in the house. First indications were the man had shot the woman then killed himself. Neighbours requested police when they heard shouting and gunfire.

He was starting to write up a report when an email arrived from Peter Garcia. The strand of hair found at Zac's house had a follicle attached which made it a cinch to gather the DNA.

```
It belongs to a Maxim Garin - there
is a file on him.
```

Mark emailed back.

```
Many thanks, Peter.
```

'Now we're getting somewhere,' Mark said out loud. He felt reenergised, enthused.

He looked into the police files and found Maxim. An image of him revealed a large, bulky man with dark complexion and a look that would engender fear in the bravest of men. He scrolled down further. Maxim was born in Russia and came to Australia eleven years ago. In time became a citizen. He was sponsored by a cousin. Mark found a file about the cousin. He had died in suspicious circumstances. The case still remained unsolved.

Maxim's records were mostly about assault. All occurred while doing his job as a part-time bouncer. Only one of them resulted in a minor charge. With other arrests he got off with a warning. He lived in Jacobie Street, Richmond.

He grabbed his partner John, who was just as enthused, and they drove to the house in Richmond.

It was a single fronted, neat and well-kept property with a flourishing front garden. They used the knocker on the front door several times, no answer. Then they drove around and found the house backed onto a lane that serviced other houses in the street. Walking the lane brought them to the rear of the property in question. Looking over the fence, they could see a man sitting at a table watching television. With a bit of strong pushing, they opened the back gate and walked across grass to the double glass door and knocked. Maxim suddenly turned in fright and ran to the front door. The detectives sprinted along the lane and around to the front, just in time to see a silver Mercedes take off with a screech down the street towards the city. They raced back to their car and took off at speed, with blue and red lights flashing. Traffic was clogged and slow but they thought they could see Maxim weaving dangerously through cars in Victoria Street.

'Christ, he's going to have an accident at this rate,' said John.

Some drivers squeezed over as best they could to let police through, but it was a tricky exercise trying to catch up. Maxim had reached Punt Road, where he went straight across against the red light. Cars crossing left and right blew car horns while pushing on their brakes in an effort to stop. One clipped his car on the back left, but he kept going. Mark and his partner stopped the pursuit; it was too dangerous. He was last seen speeding up Victoria Parade.

'Bugger it,' said Mark, slamming his hand on the wheel.

'What if we go to King Street? It can be a bit of a hangout for his type, I think he's a bouncer there, worth a try,' John suggested.

Day-time workers were spilling out of offices and zig-zagging around in different directions on their way to various forms of public transport. The detectives parked in the only space they could find. It was designated as a no parking space and was adjacent to a closed garage roller door. They saw the damaged Mercedes double parked further down the street. This area was pretty well known by the police force.

At this time of day, shadows began to crawl into laneways like a slow eclipse. It took detectives a moment to adjust their sight from the brightness of the main street. Instinctively, they spoke in whispers.

'Did you see that, Mark?'

Someone in dark clothing had briefly looked around a corner of the concrete wall, a distance down from where the detectives were standing.

'Call for back up, stay here, keep everyone away if someone tries to get in here,' said Mark.

In a low voice John phoned for support and slowly walked backward towards Mark while being ready to wave any onlookers away. Luckily no one else had entered the long laneway; they prayed no one would. Both had their guns drawn.

A shot was fired which lodged somewhere into the wall beside Mark, just missing him.

'Maxim Garin, we are the police, drop the gun and come out with your hands up. We can talk about this,' Mark said.

'Fuck you.' Maxim fired another shot, which went into the wall opposite.

It was a stalemate. Four uniforms arrived, went around the other side and came up right behind Maxim. 'This is the police, put your gun down now and hands up.'

Mark and John breathed a sigh of relief. As they walked towards the end of the lane, Maxim appeared with two strong police officers, firmly holding him by both arms and two more behind him. He was put into the police car with John and another officer either side on the back seat. Maxim wasn't going anywhere. A few pedestrians stood and watched, but not for long; these scenes were common in the city and didn't hold interest for long. Other officers arrived and cordoned off both entries to the lane.

Back at the station Maxim was put into a holding cell. An interview was to take place in fifteen minutes. Some officers stayed to watch behind the one-way glass.

At five-thirty pm Maxim was brought to the interview room. He was read his rights, then questioning commenced.

'For the record, I am Detective Mark Amos and this is my colleague Detective John Davis. This interview is being conducted with Mr Maxim Garin. Mr Garin, please state your full name, address and date of birth.'

'You're kidding me, you know *moy* name,' said Maxim. His voice was deep, and guttural. He spoke slowly, sometimes reverting to his Russian tongue.

'You are required to give your full name and address.'

Maxim sighed with impatience and spoke loudly and rapidly, acting stubborn and uncompromising. 'Maxim Garin. 55 Jacobie Street, Richmond. 3 April 1949. Satisfied? Want to know the colour of my underpants?'

'You fired two shots at police today. Why?' asked Mark.

'Because I thought you were some thugs trying to get me. I didn't know it was the police, did I?' said Maxim.

'We informed you we were police. Why would someone want to get you, Maxim?'

'Because I owe them some money, stupid – *glubby*.'

'Hey. Watch your mouth,' said Detective Davis.

'Do you understand you will be charged with a serious offence that carries a penalty of up to four years?' said Mark.

'You weren't wearing a uniform, how was I to know?'

'You know who we are, Maxim. It would help you if you can tell us where you were on Friday sixteenth May this year,' Mark said.

'Fucked if I know. Getting ready for work, I suppose. I'm a bouncer at the club on Friday nights.'

'A hair matching your DNA has been found at the premises of former Detective Zac Harris. He had been attacked and severely belted all over his body and face. What do you have to say about that, Maxim?'

'Wasn't me.'

'Your car was seen leaving the premises, Maxim,' said Mark.

'No comment.'

'You were seen visiting Mr Li in jail. Can you explain that please, Maxim?' said Mark.

The smirk left Maxim's face. 'I want a lawyer.'

'It's five forty-five. I think lawyers have left their offices for the day, don't you? Look, how about we get you a coffee and we can have a talk. You help us and we might be able to help you.'

Detective Davis came back with a coffee for everyone.

'All right, how about you tell us what happened?' said Mark with a mollifying tone of voice.

All looked at Maxim Garin. He sipped his coffee in silence then pulled out a packet of cigarettes, showed them to Mark. Mark gave a nod. Maxim lit up and dragged on his cigarette while thinking. He took a few more drags, then he spoke. 'Right, I want it mentioned in court that I was cooperative, *da*?'

'Noted,' said Mark.

'As you can see, I'm a strong man. Mr Li sometimes gets me to rough up them that owe him money or thinks they can cross him. He pays me pretty well for it. Zac stole some drugs from Li. He got them back, but Li wanted to teach him a lesson. So, I did.' Maxim was offhand in the telling with no display of remorse.

'It put him in hospital,' said Mark, who wanted to reach over the table and pummel Maxim over and over.

'*Da*, well them's the breaks,' said Maxim, nonchalantly, while stabbing out the butt of his third cigarette.

'Maxim Garin, I am charging you with the possession of an unlicensed handgun, aggravated assault and aggravated assault causing grievous bodily harm to former detective Zac Harris,' said Mark.

Maxim was read his rights and taken into custody awaiting his appearance in court.

Mark had written his report and was driving home, content Maxim was in jail. Tomorrow, Mr Li would be interviewed and charged with being complicit in the assault of Zac Harris.

He was running late for dinner. Julie was waiting for him at his father's house. Andrew and Rebecca were feeling bereft at the loss of their dog, Darling, who had died of a heart complaint a week ago.

'They could do with some company,' said Julie. 'And we need to give them the bad news about Zac. They knew and liked him too, you know.'

'Yes, of course, I'll tell them.'

It wasn't the usual rowdy dinner. There were solemn moments when Zac's decline was revealed to them.

'How could that happen? He was good at his job, had great colleagues and you, Mark, his best friend,' said Andrew.

'I've asked myself that many times, Dad. He claimed he was lonely, had one weak moment, then it became a habit which escalated out of control.'

Everyone was quiet for a moment, trying to understand the rise and fall of a man who held such promise.

'I'm sorry about your little dog, you must miss her,' said Julie, breaking the silence.

'Oh, we miss her so much. She adored us and we adored her. It's not the same around here,' said Rebecca.

'Enough with the gloom, let's get out a game. We need to have some fun. What's the choice, cards, Pictionary, Scrabble?' said Andrew, keen to change the black mood. 'I choose poker – Bec here doesn't always win at that,' he said, giving Rebecca a nudge. 'Everyone agree?'

It wasn't long before determined concentration won over gloom.

29. Melbourne

Weeks went by. Mark and Julie were out in the city, walking down Exhibition Street. It was a perfect warm night and they were looking forward to having dinner with friends at one of the more expensive restaurants. It was a birthday celebration and Julie was carrying a gift for her friend. Her husband admired her in her white, mid-length flowing, summer dress, along with her large drop earrings and high heel shoes. To him she looked like a model.

Added to the wonderful night, Mark was in a good mood. Mr Li had been charged with complicity and his incarceration had been increased by another four years. He felt justice had been served.

There were a few homeless along the street. Some were asleep, while others watched the people, hoping someone would drop some money into their containers. Both stopped to donate.

'Allo, Julie.' There was movement from under one of the covered bundles – a man poked his head further out from under his blanket. He was nearly toothless with dry, wrinkled skin.

She bent down to him. 'How you going, Billy? I haven't seen you for a while,' she said.

'Oh, yeah, I was in 'ospital, they said I had 'monia.'

'I'm sorry to hear that. Are you better now?'

'Yeah, they fixed me up. Still 'ave me dreams though, lots of weird stuff, you know?'

'Are you taking anything, Billy?'

'No, I'm off everythin'. I dream about the same fing a lot now, you know? I see a man. It's a bit dark but I can see a lot of blood over 'im. He's runnin'. Shocken.'

'Billy, that sounds like a nightmare, it's horrendous. Come and talk to me at the office. See if we can help you get off the street. Now, promise me you'll come this time. Alright?'

Mark came forward to help her up.

'Yeah, I'll come. Who's this fella?' asked Billy.

'This is my husband, Mark.'

'Good lookin' fella, you look afta her,' said Billy, with a pointed finger.

'Sure will. We have to get going now. See ya, Billy,' said Mark. 'What's his story?' asked Mark, as they walked down the street.

'Another tragedy. Parents on drugs, he was abandoned. Shifted from one well-intentioned foster family to another. He reached year twelve at school and was considered quite smart, but I don't know what happened. I think he was just a lost soul and vulnerable. The old story – turned to drugs. I see it over and over again. Don't you?'

'Yes, I do and I hate those bastards who sell the stuff,' said Mark.

The restaurant was full and noisy with countless exchanges. Each table trying to be heard above the other while waiters expertly and seamlessly weaved between tables balancing plates of cuisine. Their friends waved to them and Mark and Julie headed to the rear of the restaurant, which was mercifully quieter.

With hellos, kisses and opening of presents done, they ordered drinks and studied the menu. It was one of those restaurants that listed high prices. Mark and Julie were not concerned. For them this was a rare outing at an exclusive venue. To hell with the cost.

They had the best of nights. It was about one in the morning when they walked past Billy, who was asleep.

'Will he come and see you?' asked Mark.

'Possibly not. He does sometimes but it's rare. It can be tortuous tying to help someone who is used to living on the streets. Some of them get so used to it they like it that way.'

Driving home their talk was about the superb food, fantastic company and scintillating exchanges on a range of topics.

'Oh … shit, shit, shit,' said Mark, in the middle of a pause.

'What?'

'Billy, Billy!' he exclaimed.

'What about him?'

'The dream he keeps having, the dream he was talking about.'

'What about it?'

'He could be describing the man in the lane; bloody hell, I think he saw him.'

'The body you found, you mean? That was a few months ago, wasn't it? Hasn't he been identified yet?' Julie asked.

'No and I would like to bet Billy has witnessed this man running to the lane. I have to go back and see him, ask him more.'

'Not now, Mark, please.'

'No, of course, not now, but tomorrow? Is he always in the same spot?'

'I don't know. I'm under the impression he moves around a lot during the day. You would have more luck at dusk. Saturday night is busy, lots of people. He may be sitting there hoping to have more money thrown into his open cap,' said Julie.

'Will you come with me?'

'If you think it would help, yes, sure.'

'So far, we have hit a colossal wall with this case. It's worth asking. What gets me is no one reported it. Others must have seen him,' Mark said.

'People turn a blind eye. Likely as not, they thought he was just some mad street person and didn't want to become involved. It's a reflection on society unfortunately. They have little sympathy for those on the street. A few just drop a couple of coins then walk away without any concern or interest about the person, how they came to be in that position.'

Mark was lying in bed looking up to the ceiling, deep in thought. Julie was sleeping soundly. Of all the cases he had investigated, the man in the lane disturbed him the most. There was something poignant about seeing him lying there, naked, in the foetal position, wet, bloodied, severely injured and completely alone. *No one should die like that*, he thought.

He tried to sleep for two hours. Exasperated, he got up and made a coffee. His sleeplessness was due to anticipation. He couldn't get Billy out of his head. *It might be he knows something, witnessed something.* Mark sat on the couch and turned on the TV, surrendering the idea of sleep.

Next evening, Mark and Julie walked down Exhibition Street. Mark began to feel the effects of his lack of sleep the night before. His eyes were stinging. As envisaged, there were people everywhere, going off to their particular place of entertainment. Most ignored the homeless but a few contributed some coins.

'There he is.' Julie came up to him and squatted down, level with his face. 'Hi, Billy, how you going?'

''Allo, love. Ya back out again? What ya doing tonight?'

'Billy, I have a favour to ask. Do you remember my husband here, Mark? She pulled Mark down beside her.

'Yeah, good lookin' fella, how ya goin'?' He offered a hand to Mark. Mark held on to Billy's rough fingers.

'Now don't be afraid, Billy. You haven't done anything wrong. Mark is a detective and only wants to ask you something.'

'I haven't done anythin', 'ave I?' Billy looked at Julie for reassurance.

'No, Billy, you are not in any trouble,' said Mark, who now held Billy's hand in both of his. 'I want to ask you about your dream, okay?'

Billy nodded.

'You said you have dreams about a man running with no clothes on and has blood on him. Is that right?'

'Yeah, shocken. It keeps comin' into me head, ya know?'

'I understand, it must be horrible for you. Billy, in your dream, do you see where he came from or where he went?' Mark held his breath, hoping.

'Yeah. In me dream I see 'im comin' from over there.' Billy lifted his other hand and pointed to a structure on the other side of the street, a few doors down from where he was sitting.

Mark's heart started pounding. 'Thank you very much, Billy, you have been a great help. You may have solved a big problem for me.'

'Ave I helped the cops then?' Billy said with pride.

'You have, Billy, thank you. We will go and have a look now.' Mark pulled out a twenty-dollar note and handed it to him.

'Ya don't 'av<u>e</u> to do that but fanks. I'm runnin' a bit low,' said Billy.

'Promise you'll come and see me,' said Julie.

Billy confirmed he would.

'What a waste. I can see a glimmer of what could have been. I hope you can do something for him,' said Mark, as they hurried down the street.

'I'll do my best. Keep in mind he has to want to be helped,' said Julie.

They reached the area Billy had pointed to. A red, weathered, expansive timber door, like the kind seen in the suburbs, the type that covered a double garage. The building looked out of place. The rest of the street consisted of shops and restaurants. The doors had a large padlock holding it securely closed. Mark rattled it but it wouldn't budge. He knew he wouldn't be able to access the interior without permission anyway. Reluctantly, they left the scene. He would deal with it first thing in the morning.

As they walked back, they could see Billy over the other side of the street, accepting some coins from a passer-by.

'Bless you, Billy,' whispered Mark. 'I hope you have the very best of luck.'

Julie put her arm through his as they hurried back home. Mark was back at the station in the detective senior sergeant's office. He requested a warrant to search the premises in Exhibition Street and gave his reasons. A search also disclosed the name and contact details of the owner of the warehouse: a Mr Wayne Salter who had another warehouse in South Melbourne. A search found he had never had any dealings with the police. No charges or investigations. Mark called him, advised him of their suspicions and asked if he could attend the breaking in of the building and be a witness to the police search. This would corroborate police activities and reduce any allegations of an improper search. Surprise and shock were evident in his shaking voice as he agreed to meet at the address.

With warrant in hand, Mark went to the property with Detective John Davis, four other officers and the middle-aged Mr Salter, the owner, who was still shaken. Three police cars were parked in the street attracting the usual stares from passers-by. One officer skilfully broke the large padlock with bolt cutters, pulled open the wide doors and walked into the spacious warehouse. Mr Salter stood on the footpath outside watching on. A police officer was with him to keep onlookers at bay.

It was dark and mostly windowless except for two narrow, long slits of glass high above a side wall. It had a mouldy odour and the beams of torchlight exposed a high ceiling covered in cobwebs. Detective Davis found a light switch and a few fluorescent tubes gradually came to life. The police, clad in gloves and foot coverings, moved cautiously through the building, some focusing on the floor, some continuing to shine their torches on the ceiling. Different sized cardboard boxes were stored haphazardly against exposed, studded, brick walls. One of the officers shouted out saying he'd found some blood on the floor, spots of it here and there. Another officer found a wooden chair on its side against the back brick wall. It also had some blood on the armrests.

'Get forensics here, please,' said Mark to the officer. 'I think maybe this is where it happened.'

'What? You mean the guy in the lane?' asked Detective Davis.

Just before he could answer, an officer came towards him with a wooden baseball bat. It had smears of blood on the handle, barrel and end.

'And that, my man, is a yes,' said Mark. He took the bat and stood completely still, holding the top with a finger and thumb, as if in a trance.

Peter arrived within ten minutes.

'You can let it go now; we'll take care of it,' he said to Mark.

'Yeah, right, thanks, Peter. This is a precious piece of evidence.'

'I know what this means to you. We'll get info to you as speedily as we can. Now, let's do some dusting for prints, shall we?' He walked away with his assistant.

Mark directed officers to inspect the numerous boxes stacked up on either side of the building. Inside were packs of Chinese noodles and other paraphernalia to do with the running of a restaurant. No trace of drugs.

Peter Garcia came up to Mark. 'Right, we've gathered what we need from here. We'll be off. And before you ask, we'll make it a priority,' said Peter.

When the police had finished, the large doors were securely locked and police tapes spread across the front. Mark spoke with Wayne Salter.

'Tests will need to be done to confirm it, but we think a crime has been committed here, Mr Salter. It's going to take a while before you can get in there and clear it out or do whatever you want to. You need to know your tenant, Mr Li, is already in jail on another matter. I'm assuming you know nothing about this?'

'Oh my god. No, please, this is a terrible shock. I never had any worry about Mr Li. I've only been here a couple of times to check on things and Li was always cooperative and helpful. I don't know what this is about, but whatever it is, I'm surprised and stunned. What sort of crime are we talking here?'

'I can't say at this stage but it's serious, Mr Salter. We will keep you up-to-date. Here's my card. Ring me anytime. I'll give you answers where I can. What will you do about the warehouse?'

'Sell it, I think. I don't want it keep now, especially if something terrible has happened within those walls. I have another, as you probably know. These buildings are meant to be my superannuation.' He shook hands with Mark and thanked him. Wayne Salter's head was bent low as he walked away. Now and then he shook it from side to side.

It's going to take him a while to get over this, thought Mark. Results from forensic examinations were in and detectives were ordered in for a briefing. With the meeting over, Detectives Mark Amos, John Davis and two detectives from the drug squad made their way to the prison to interview Mr Li and Maxim Garin.

30. Melbourne

Two unmarked police cars turned into the parking area of the prison. Prison officers had confirmed Mr Li and Maxim Garin were ready for their interviews. With checks completed the detectives separated – drug squad to one interview room and homicide detectives to another. Both would have a video recording of the proceedings.

Maxim came into the room, handcuffed, accompanied by a prison officer who went and stood at the rear of the room. He'd put on weight, which made him look more threatening and he sported a black eye.

'You should see the other guy,' he said, with a menacing grin. His voice sounded deeper and slower than in previous interviews. It hadn't lost its Russian tone or gained any of the jail vernacular.

With the standard who's who in the room and confirmation of the prisoner's name and address for the video recording, Mark then looked straight into Maxim's eyes. He began with friendly banter, wanting to ease the prisoner into a genial conversation. Make him comfortable to talk and, with any luck, confess. 'You're looking well, Maxim. Prison agrees with you.'

'Yeah, well, food's not bad, I suppose. Company is pretty shit though.' He chuckled, thinking himself amusing.

'Tell me something, Maxim. I've wondered; why did you leave your native Russia and come to this country?' asked Mark.

'Why do you want to know?' Maxim was startled at the line of questioning.

'I'm interested.'

Maxim sat back in the chair, ready to tell his story. Nobody had ever asked him this before. He bent his head down slightly. 'My mother is dead and my father was a very, very bad man. He beat me. I had to get away, *da*.'

'I see. Not a good start in life then.' Mark still couldn't find it in his heart to feel pity for this man.

'I'll get straight to the point. Tell us where you were on Tuesday the fourteenth April this year?'

'For Christ's sake. How am I supposed to remember that?' He became pugnacious. 'Look, *moy* life is the same every day, right? I do some bouncer work at the clubs or whatever, I come home, eat, sleep and go back next afternoon. That's it.'

'Pretty expensive house and car for part-time work, wouldn't you say?' said Mark.

Maxim leaned his face closer to Mark. 'Ever heard of saving your money?' he said with sneering sarcasm.

'Sit back, Maxim,' warned the officer from the back of the room.

'You also do some work for Mr Li. You said in a previous statement you are employed by him to *"rough some people up"*. Is that correct, Maxim?'

'Listen, I'm in here for a job I only did once, all right, just once. Usually I give a warning, nothing else, *da*? Your mate

Harris got a bit too smart. He hit me first, *da*, he hit me first.' Maxim was becoming uneasy, shifting his large frame in the chair.

'Detectives, police officers and a forensic officer have thoroughly inspected a warehouse in Exhibition Street. Your fingerprints are everywhere in that place. Can you explain that, Maxim?' Mark asked casually, while looking down at his pad.

'Do I need a lawyer?' asked Maxim.

'Up to you. Can you explain why your finger prints are in the warehouse?'

He paused, then, 'I'd go there a lot of the time for Mr Li. You know, take deliveries, stocktake, that kinda stuff. He rents the place.'

'I see. Can you explain why your fingerprints are on a baseball bat left at the scene?'

'I dunno. I don't own a bat. Why would I have a baseball bat? Do I look like someone who runs around in a circle on the grass or something? I mean, look at me,' he said, pointing at his rounded stomach. 'I'm not that fit, I'm just big.' He tut-tutted nervously while shifting in his chair again.

'A splinter was found in the skull of a dead man that matches the same baseball bat found at that scene. Officers also found a smear of your blood on a chair in the warehouse. Can you tell us about that?'

'No comment. I want *moy* lawyer.'

'You were wearing rings on your fingers when you were first brought into the station. Where are they now?'

'The prison bloke took them. I'm not allowed to wear them in here. They'd better be with *moy* stuff when I get out,' said Maxim, in an attempt to revive his diminishing bravado.

'There's a lot of evidence placing you at that warehouse, Maxim. There is indisputable evidence of your blood on the bat, the chair and other places in that building. Now, it would be in your interests to tell us what happened,' said Mark.

'What do you mean, in *moy* interests?'

'In my experience, courts look more favourably on someone who has cooperated,' said Mark, hoping this would encourage a confession.

There was a pause; the room went eerily quiet. Then Maxim spoke. 'Can I smoke?'

Mark looked up at the officer standing at the back of the room and gave him a nod. The officer came back with a packet of cigarettes and a tin foil ashtray.

The video recording recommenced. Maxim hungrily put a cigarette to his mouth with his cuffed hands and drew the smoke deep into his lungs. Officers in the room stayed silent and didn't move. No one wanted to disturb this moment and risk a long-awaited confession.

Maxim finished one cigarette then lit another. 'He owed us a lot of money, a lot of money,' he said.

'Who is us?' said Mark.

'Me and Li. Our lawyer owed us big time. He bloody disappeared by the way. We got most of the money back though. He posted it. Can you believe it? I got his son, you see; I couldn't get to him, but I got his son. Must have scared him cause the money came back all right. Thieving bastard.' Maxim was rambling, talking to himself while looking at the ceiling, blowing cigarette smoke.

'How did you know it was his son?'

'I went to see the prick. Told him to get our money back. The scum told me his son was coming right then to meet him and I had to leave straight away. Said he would fix up everything as soon as possible. I passed his son on the stairs. Couldn't miss him, he looked like his father. I waited across the road outta sight. They came out of the building together, you see, so I followed them to Chinatown. They went in to eat or something. They were there for a bloody long time. I kept waiting. His son came out first so I followed him. He was doing a bit of looking around and ended up in Exhibition Street. It was getting dark. I went inside the warehouse and stood inside near the door of the building, looking out, watching him. I'd already left the door unlocked because I hadn't finished unpacking a delivery. Just as he came near the warehouse, I pulled him in with one hand and slammed the door shut with the other. I'm strong, you see. He didn't know what hit him. I knocked him out straight away, then I dragged him to a chair down the back. He woke up and I told him to take his clothes off and give me his wallet. I knew he wouldn't run away without his clothes and wallet. He thought I was just going to rob him. At first he refused, so I whacked him. He was a pretty strong bloke, but not a match for me. Then I made him sit down again. He kept on asking me what I wanted; said I must have the wrong person. So I told him what this was about. He looked a bit shocked, I have to say. I gave him some cigarette burns to start with. Then I gave him a few cuts with a knife. He yelled out a bit, then he tried to fight me. That makes me mad, you know? I kept whacking him with *moy* bat. In the end I just dropped the bat and left. He was well and truly out to it and I wanted a break. I had to call the club, tell them I wouldn't be in, then I went for a drink, I needed a couple by then. I was away for … I dunno, an hour or so maybe. When I got back, he was bloody gone. I mean, how'd he do that? He was half dead when I last saw him. I should have locked that fuckin' door.'

Those in the room thought they had seen and heard it all but the aggressiveness and lack of compassion from this man horrified them. Faces of the officers reddened and their breathing became rapid. Mark kept his rage in check.

'I'm wondering why no one heard anything,' Mark said.

'Ya can't hear nothing with the doors closed and you're right at the back,' said Maxim.

'Go on,' said Mark.

'Not much else to say. I started looking around the streets. I kept thinking he couldn't have gone far. Christ, he was pretty banged up. I was going to give up, then I found him down a lane up the street, nearly didn't look there. He was curled up like a baby but still breathing, just, so I left him. Went back and cleaned up as much as I could about the place. I hid the bat and wiped the chair. Not enough though, but I didn't stress then, didn't expect anyone would be looking in there, no way. No one would know what had happened, would they? I mean he wasn't going to say anything by then, was he?'

'What did you do with his clothes?

'I took them back home and burnt them. Burnt everything. I've got an old 'cinerator,' said Maxim.

'Did he have a wallet? If he did, surely his details were in there?'

'Yeah, he did, but I didn't look much at that. There was a couple of thousand in it, so I took that out and burnt the rest. Look, his father's name is Hughe Smyth. As I said, he's our lawyer, has a few fancy letters with his name, ask him. I haven't seen him since, don't know where he is. I do know one thing; he won't rob us again,' said Maxim, who didn't seem to comprehend the seriousness of what he had done. By now Maxim had smoked half a packet of cigarettes. He asked for water.

'We'll finish here, Maxim. We will need to talk to you again,' said Mark.

'Yeah, you do that. I'll have *moy* lawyer with me then.'

The two detectives went into a spare room. The officer who had recorded the interview followed them. There was nothing they could say that would explain what they had just heard. Silence prevailed until detectives from the drug squad joined them.

'You guys looked exhausted,' said the drug squad detective.

'Anything from Li?' Mark asked.

'Nope, only thing we could get out of him was, "I not know anything, someone kill me," and, "Mr Garin works in warehouse for my restaurant". That was it, despite the many times or different ways we questioned him.'

Mark then told them of the interview with Maxim. All they could do was shake their heads in disbelief.

It was established nothing would be gained by continuing more interviews that day, so they went back to the station. With reports completed, officers went out for a drink together. They needed a release from the barbarity they heard that day. None of them could come up with any answers. *What made Maxim into the monster he had become?* Talk went back and forth. A couple of officers proffered the nurture-nature theory, among others. But none of it gave them the definitive answer they were searching for.

31. Melbourne

Detective Senior Sergeant Morris put down the phone. He felt for the Smyths, most poignantly Eric, as it had been difficult to convey what had happened to Gary. He asked Eric Smyth if he could come to Melbourne as police wanted to give him a briefing about his brother.

Next day, Eric arrived at the police station. It was his first meeting with Mark Amos. They were both waiting in the office of the detective senior sergeant. A faint whiff of aftershave pervaded the air, and the sun was coming through the windows, glowing down onto a clean, tidy office. A few large volumes stood on the shelf of a modest bookcase, along with a family photo, another of the detective senior sergeant having something pinned to his uniform by an officer and two trophies.

The middle-aged senior sergeant entered the room, slightly out of breath and apologised for being late. He was tall with a kindly face and styled greying hair. He looked distinguished, authoritative and resplendent in a spotless uniform. Introductions done, the three men sat and Detective Senior Sergeant Morris opened the only file on his desk.

'Eric, I am here to tell you we think we have found your brother.'

'And?'

'It is with deep regret I have to tell you, if it is your brother, he is deceased.'

Eric dropped his head momentarily. 'How did it happen?'

Mark conveyed what they now knew, leaving out some of the more gruesome findings. 'Li and Garin have been charged. They have both confessed to their involvement in the death of this person. We have no doubt, when tried they will stay in jail for a long time, Eric. I know that doesn't make it any less painful but at least we've got them. The other thing is we need to confirm his identity. Are you prepared to come to the morgue to do that?'

'Yes, yes, I am.'

'Eric, I need to warn you. He was severely beaten. It may be that you will be unable to positively identify him. If you can't, we could do so by a DNA test. What do you want to do?'

'I want to see him first. I have to see him, it's very important to me.'

'We understand. I will be with you, but would you also like to have a minister of the church accompany you?' Mark asked.

'Thank you, but I should be all right.'

Arriving at the mortuary, Eric was taken to a room where Gary's body lay on a trolley covered in a clean white sheet. Mark stood by.

Peter Garcia was standing beside the viewing screen waiting. 'Hello, Eric. I'm Peter Garcia, forensic pathologist. You can stand out here if you would prefer. However, if you find you need to look more closely, we can bring you nearer to him. I need to inform you that, though this man has been refrigerated, he has decomposed to a certain degree. Do you still wish to view him?'

'Yes, I do please,' said Eric.

'Very well.' Peter went back to the trolley and slowly pulled back the sheet to reveal Gary's face. He had purposely positioned the side of the face that was more intact.

Eric turned away for a moment and Mark came forward to support him. 'Are you all right, Eric?'

'Yes, yes, thanks, Mark. That was harrowing, but I'm all right.'

Eric turned back and concentrated on the shrunken face. He asked to come in and look more closely. The hair was Gary's. The injuries to his face distorted the way he looked, but Eric was able identify the body as that of his brother, Gary. He stood looking down at him for some time, crying. 'He has a brown mole on his back near his left shoulder. Could you confirm that for me please? Just so there is absolutely no doubt.'

'Of course,' said Peter. He folded the sheet back just enough to reveal the shoulder to Eric. The mole was visible.

'Yes, that's him. This is definitely my brother, Gary Smyth. I was hoping it wasn't, but it is.' Eric was obviously distressed. 'Thank you, Peter.'

Eric was composing himself while being driven back to the station. Forms had to be completed and questions answered.

'The family always held out some hope. My mother predicted he was dead. She's more pragmatic than the rest of us. I'm struggling to come to terms with what happened as you described, Mark. I mean, who would do such a thing?'

'Some very greedy, desperate individuals, Eric. Money and drugs have a way of dehumanising them. They end up losing their sense of decency. Your brother was in the wrong place at the wrong time. I'm sorry this has happened to your family.'

'He wasn't the only victim.' Eric told Mark how his father had died.

When he left, Mark reflected on Eric's demeanour. He was a long-limbed, handsome man, imbued with a fine intelligence, softly spoken and cultivated. He strode with quiet, measured movements. Now, he was thrust into the dark world of criminals and drugs, a world that was totally foreign to him. How does such a man deal with loss caused by suicide and callous brutality? Mark wondered if he felt the same as he did when his friend Zac walked down that same path – that feeling of overwhelming helplessness.

32. Hobart

On the plane travelling back to Hobart, Eric was thinking of the best way to tell his mother how Gary had died. Gary's body was to be released by the coroner and the funeral parlour would make arrangements for his body to be sent back home. He didn't want her to see him; he would prevent it. It would be far too shocking for her to handle. Better that she remembered him from the photos she had.

Cynthia and his daughters were at the airport to meet him.

'You sounded so fretful on the phone darling.' Cynthia held him tightly and kissed his face. She linked his arm with hers as they walked towards the car. She felt it essential to remind him how much he was loved and supported. It was obvious he was suffering.

'I still am. It's like being in a bad dream. Did you contact Richard?'

'Yes. Both Gary's places were rented so any monies owing will, at most, only be for a few months rent. He wanted to know what to do with his Land Rover and other personal items. He asked if he could drive it down here, pack it up with some of Gary's stuff. Very kind, I thought.'

'Yes, it is. I think we should leave it up to him. It's a long way. He can keep the Land Rover and any furniture or whatever if he wants. Just post the personal things. I'll ring him,' said Eric.

His wife and girls comforted him with hugs and affection. Being back home calmed him and reinforced how fortunate he was to have his family. 'If only Dad and Gary could see you and my wonderful girls,' he lamented. It started a flow of tears again. It was the first time his daughters had seen their father cry.

Eric was sitting on Imogen's lounge and she was pouring tea from her treasured teapot. Eric found it obscene considering the real cost of her inanimate possessions. He had an urge to hit her across the face, wake her up from her stupid preoccupations, her absolute need to be admired, to be noticed, to be envied. He resisted the temptation and instead spoke calmly. 'Mum, I have news about Gary.'

'Oh, where is he?'

'He's dead, Mum.'

She remained steadfast and held on to her teapot. 'So, I was right then. Are you going to tell me how he died?' Imogen asked as she handed him a cup of tea. Her steady voice and mannerisms gave nothing away about how she received the news.

'It wasn't from an unfortunate accident or illness or anything like that he … he was murdered.'

'Why would anyone want to murder Gary?' she asked with raised eyebrows.

'He was murdered by a very brutish man. This man was a hired criminal and assaulted Gary on behalf of the clients Dad had stolen money from. Gary was bludgeoned so severely he died, by himself, curled up in a laneway near Exhibition

Street. This mongrel was an opportunist. He knew Dad and Gary were having lunch together. He followed and waited until Gary was alone, like an animal about to pounce on easy prey. Then he dragged Gary into a warehouse and beat him senseless. Somehow, Gary was able to run away and make it to the lane. I can only assume it was due to his supreme fitness that enabled him to make it that far. The men who are responsible for this are now in jail.' He was growing angry as he related all to his mother.

Imogen was stunned. She looked down to the floor for a moment then back at Eric, her faced pained. 'When is he coming home?' she asked.

'In a few days,' he answered brusquely.

'Don't be angry, dear. None of us could know this would happen. If anything, I thought he would come to harm while travelling in the outback on his own.'

Eric stood up; he could no longer hold is rage. He removed the teapot then upended the low, occasional table. Most of the crockery fell to the floor. He picked up as many pieces as he could hold, took them out the back door and, in a frenzy, smashed them to bits. He came back, grabbed the teapot, one of his mother's most coveted pieces, and smashed it to smithereens. Imogen screamed out.

'Please, Eric, stop it, what are you doing? That is my very best teapot, my very best cups, please, please, don't do this.' She grabbed him as he came back through the door.

'Was every piece of those *very best things* worth it, Mum? Were they?'

'You're frightening me, Eric, what's wrong with you?'

He ran out the front door, got into his car and pushed the accelerator right to the floor. He had to get away from her. Years of supressed anger and pain had risen to the surface like bubbling hot lava. To him, his mother was to blame for the senseless death of a beloved father and brother. At that moment he hated her more than ever and never wanted see her again.

Gary's body was lying at a funeral parlour located in Letitia Street, North Hobart. Johnathan stood with him while Cynthia stood back. She didn't want to view the body. Imogen had been strongly dissuaded from coming. For once, she acquiesced.

The parlour staff had prepared his body with makeup, his hair was combed and his face and body had been injected with preservatives. His eyes and mouth were closed. All the caring preparation done by staff created a man who looked a bit more familiar, like the Gary that Eric had known. Some clothing had been supplied for him to wear and a ring Gary wore was given back to the family.

The family gathered at the service for his cremation. He would be placed not far from his father with a plaque stating his name and those he was related to.

Richard had driven down from Alice Springs. He wanted to attend the funeral and hand over whatever the family wanted to keep.

Afternoon tea at Eric's home had finished. Focus was now on sorting through Gary's things. He kept a diary of his travels and dozens of photos showing his pleasing, wide smile surrounded by happy people he had taken on camping trips. There were varying poses with arms folded around shoulders. The group were wearing wide-brimmed hats and sporting outback dust over their clothes. Among the photos was one of him and Rebecca Parke on their wedding day. They both looked so young and happy.

'He loved his life. Taking others to see the grandeur of the desert and vastness of Australia was a dream job for him,' said Richard.

'To our dear Gary, may he continue his wanderings in another peaceful place,' said Eric.

Glasses were lifted. 'To Gary,' they all said in unison. People started mingling.

Eric came up to Gary's partner from the Northern Territory. 'Thank you, Richard, for coming. It's a long way, then you had to come across by boat as well. You must have liked him a lot.'

'He was a trusted mate and I admired him. It was a gutsy move to leave a comfortable teaching job to do what he did. I'll miss him,' said Richard.

'Can you stay with us for a while? We have a spare room, you are most welcome,' said Eric.

'If you don't mind, I'd love to.'

Richard stayed for a week and explored Hobart and surrounds, then it was time for him to go. It was decided he would keep the Land Rover and anything else of Gary's that remained back at Alice.

'Maybe I'll give up my full-time job and take up where Gary left off.'

'That sounds like a very good plan. Please keep in touch. We would like to come and camp with you one day. We haven't seen Alice Springs.'

It was a week after Gary's funeral. The girls were at school and Cynthia had resumed working. Eric was in the middle of practising a piece for the upcoming Hobart Symphony concert when the phone rang. Imogen had just been admitted to the Royal Hobart Hospital and could he come as soon as possible please.

While at the hospital, Eric found out that Imogen's one and only friend had gone to visit. They had morning tea together every Wednesday. When her constant knocking wasn't answered she went to the back door. It was open and she had found Imogen on the floor unable to move or speak.

'She has had a stroke. She will improve, but by how much we don't know just yet. She will most likely need rehabilitation for some time to come. Do you have room and facilities at home for her?' asked her doctor.

'No,' said Eric, a bit too hastily. He did not want her to come back to his place. It was out of the question.

'I can recommend an excellent home-based provider. If she can do the basics, walking et cetera, she can go home,' said the doctor.

Imogen was back in three weeks and was receiving attention from home-care on a daily basis, along with an exercise plan with a visiting physiotherapist. She could walk with a stick and do most things, but her speech was impaired and her left arm was immobile. Cynthia came to her at the end of each work day and Eric would spend at least one day of the weekend with her. She had aged considerably. Her hair was snow white; she no longer wore her makeup.

One Sunday, while Eric was talking to her, she collapsed. He rang for an ambulance and tried to revive her until they came. Her eyes were open but there was no response. Her heart had stopped. He gave her CPR. Nothing. The ambulance officers continued with CPR while she was being driven to hospital, but it was too late. Imogen had died.

Eric, his family, Johnathan Lewis, a few members of the orchestra and one of Imogen's friends were at Cornelian Bay Cemetery for Imogen's burial. Everyone else she knew had melted away long ago. There was no room for her ashes to have a separate cavity next to Hughe in the red brick cemetery structure, so it was agreed she could be put in with her husband and the plaque would be changed to include her name. Imogen's house was sold and some of the contents either given away or kept.

One day, with practice done, Eric was sitting outside with a coffee. His mind went back to the tragic end to the life of his father and Gary. Although he was no longer bitter, he could never feel love for his mother. Her desperate needs brought ruin to the whole family.

But he was still alive with his wonderful wife and girls. He knew how fortunate he was. He and Cynthia were going on a camping trip to Alice Springs when the girls were older. The girls were thrilled they would have the house to themselves during those couple of weeks. Richard would prepare a trip and take them to some of the places where Gary used to camp. Eric was looking forward to that.

33. Melbourne

Detective Mark Amos had just hung up from speaking with Eric Smyth. He advised that Maxim Garin had been sentenced for a non-parole period of twenty years for the manslaughter of Gary Smyth in addition to the sentence he was already serving for the grievous bodily harm to Homicide Detective Zac Harris.

Mr Li was sentenced to eighteen years for complicity to the manslaughter of Gary Smyth in addition to the sentence he was already serving for complicity in the aggravated assault of Homicide Detective Zac Harris, drug possession and distribution of a prohibited drug.

'They will most probably die in jail, Eric. Neither is young and they are going to be in there for a long time. Nothing will bring Gary back, but I hope you feel justice has been done.'

Just as the conversation was coming to an end, Eric invited Mark and his wife to come and stay one day. They would enjoy Hobart. 'Thanks, Eric, we'll take you up on that.'

It was the end of the day and Mark was on his way to visit Rebecca. Julie had gone to visit her mother who was unwell and his dad was at the local Living and Learning centre on a session about beekeeping. 'Of all things,' Rebecca had said.

He knocked on the half open front door. Suddenly, a little white puppy appeared and came running and slipping up the hallway to greet him. It barked a puppy bark in defence of the house. When in his arms, it vigorously licked Mark's face. Rebecca came up to greet him, giving him a kiss on the cheek and taking the dog from him.

'When did this happen?' he asked, delighted by the surprise.

'I know, I know. We said we never would again when Darling died, but a friend who breeds them brought her around. Said we could have her if we wanted. Our hearts melted immediately. She chews our shoes and slippers and toilet training is not quite there but … thank God for a doggy door.'

'What have you named her?'

'Bonnie because she's a bonny girl. Bit cliché but we like it and so does she.'

'I brought the wine. If you can supply the glasses, we can sit out on the balcony and have a drink. What do you think?'

'Good idea. What's this about? You have something to tell me, you said.'

'Yes, I do. Let's settle in first.'

They each had a drink and were sitting outside in the cool still air.

'Now I know we have given up, but I think, on this occasion, it's needed. Two for you and two for me.' Mark gave her a cigarette and they both lit up.

'Phew, it's been a while,' said Rebecca.

'It's a bit naughty. I was glad when you said Dad wouldn't be here.' Mark laughed. 'Now, I remember you talking about some snobby people once. The Smyths, is that right?'

'Oh, the Smyths, yes. I was married to their son Gary for about two years. Bit of a disaster. Wow, that was a long time ago. Why? Do you know them?'

'You might read something in the paper one day, or an edited version of it. I want to give you the whole story first.'

'This sounds like some interesting gossip, do tell,' said Rebecca.

'Recently, in the early hours of the morning, Zac and I were attending a scene to investigate a dead body of a man in a lane just off Exhibition Street ...'

An hour and a half had passed before Mark had finished. Andrew came home to the smell of cigarette smoke and Rebecca sitting in the chair holding on tightly to Bonnie.

'I'll go and see them,' she said to Mark.

'I'm sure they would welcome it.' He looked around to see his father. 'Hi, Dad.'

'What's going on?' said Andrew, who was affronted by cigarette smoke.

'Grab a drink, Dad, I have some news.'

34. Hobart

Rebecca flew back to her hometown with mixed feelings. Andrew agreed this was a journey best suited just for her. She loved him for his understanding and insight for her need to do things on her own. 'I'm blessed to have someone like you,' she had once told him.

She booked a room in Hadley's Hotel, the same hotel where Tim had proposed marriage to her. Rebecca didn't want the same room, figuring that would become too sentimental. Inevitably though, staying there brought back a flood of memories. She looked out the window, thinking of him and paying her own private homage. He would never be forgotten, but years had passed and memories of him came less often. The accident that killed him was replaced by sweeter thoughts.

There was apprehension about contacting Eric Smyth. His brother had died a horrible death. She fretted that he would be disinclined to talk to his former sister-in-law. Rebecca and Gary hadn't been together for many years. Not that the separation and inevitable divorce was her choice. Then, of course, there was the unfortunate interaction with their mother, Imogen. Rebecca expected some modicum of sympathy from her considering the total abandonment of the marriage by Imogen's son. She had pleaded with Imogen to help to save the marriage, help her understand what Gary wanted from it. Instead, she had received a cup of tea from Imogen's best china, served with an air of superiority and some meaningless tut-tutting about her favourite son.

'He's rather a naughty boy sometimes. He did tell me he was going, wanted to be doing something outdoors. He's on his way already,' Imogen had said with obvious pride.

In a rage Rebecca had said something akin to Imogen's facile mind, threw her wedding rings at Imogen and walked out. Did Imogen relay that altercation to her sons?

Rebecca should have rung first, let Eric know she was coming. But she didn't want to talk to him over the phone. Rebecca wanted to meet with him. It had always been her way – deal with things face-to-face. She wanted to express her sympathy for the horrible way Gary had died, to say how sorry she was for the loss of his brother. She was unsure about mentioning his father and mother. *See how this turns out today*, she thought.

Rebecca had found their address in a box among some photographs. She now stood waiting at the front door of his home, having first given a gentle knock. A piano was being played in the house. She waited a minute then knocked again, more loudly than the first.

An attractive woman opened the door. The music continued to be played. It sounded like a classical piece, the playing beautiful.

'Hello, can I help you?'

'Sorry to disturb you, we haven't met before. I'm Rebecca, Kathleen and Harold Whitman's granddaughter. I was once married to Gary. I wanted to come and give my sincere condolences in person.' She was surprised at her own nervousness.

'Oh, my goodness. Well, welcome, please come in.'

'Thank you,' Rebecca said, while still feeling awkward.

'I'm Cynthia, Eric's wife,' she said with a generous smile. 'Eric, Eric, there's someone here to see you.' She guided Rebecca to the lounge room.

Eric immediately stopped playing and walked into the room. Rebecca had forgotten how tall he was. He stopped for a moment and looked at her. Then recognition spread over his face.

'My dear Rebecca, how wonderful to see you, it's been a long time. I—'

Rebecca interrupted. 'I hope you don't mind me turning up like this but I wanted to tell you how sorry I am about Gary.'

'How did you know?' He was astonished.

'Detective Mark Amos is my stepson. As you know, he solved the case. He remembered Gary and I had been married a long time ago and wanted to tell me about it before it became public. That is, in case it became public. Hope you don't mind.'

'No, no, of course not. It's kind of you to come and see us. Goodness, you haven't changed a bit, you know. What can we get you? Would you like some tea or coffee?'

'Well, thank you, and a cup of tea would be lovely.' Rebecca was invited to sit down. She felt welcomed and relaxed. Misgivings vanished.

Cynthia served cups of tea accompanied by cake and they sat and talked about many things, including how Hughe had died. Imogen wasn't mentioned. There was much to say and they compared stories long into late afternoon.

In a brief moment of silence, Eric suddenly jumped up and asked Rebecca if she would like to see some photos of Gary.

'Yes, I would,' she said, while not being sure if she did or not.

He brought out a box and started sorting through some photos he thought she might like to see. There was Gary accompanied with his charges out in the desert, everyone sporting wide smiles. There was some of him standing alone with a large hat on his head, almost covering his face. His large grin dominated every image and, although their parting was acrimonious, she felt moved. His life should not have ended like it did. He deserved much better.

Eric tenderly handed her the last photo in the group. It was more tattered around the edges than the others and starting to yellow.

'Look at the comment on the back.' He studied Rebecca, waiting for her reaction.

The one that got away, my fault.

She looked up at Eric. 'I didn't run away, you know, he left me because he was bored. As you can see, he was much happier being out in the desert.'

'Oh, yes, we realise that. I wanted you to know he had regrets about leaving you behind.'

Rebecca put her arms around Eric. 'Thank you, Eric, I'm glad you showed me.'

'Would you like to have it, perhaps?'

She thought for a minute. Did she want it? Then she said yes. Andrew wouldn't mind; it was part of her history. She would add it to the box of photos of her past. It would become part of those who she once loved and were now gone. Sometimes, she revisited those years.

It was time to go. Eric and Cynthia showed her to the door, hugged and kissed her goodbye and thanked her for thinking of them, inviting her back whenever she wanted.

She had dinner at the hotel. Back in her room she called Andrew and told him of her day.

Rebecca took advantage of time left the following morning and went down to Taroona. Driving down the steep street was a bittersweet moment.

Kathleen and Harold's house still stood although some changes had been made. It had a new coat of paint and there was a basketball hoop over the garage. The garden was as it had always been. It looked well tended. She was happy to see it still survived.

She stepped out of the car and changed to flat shoes to enable her to navigate the steep track. Instead of dirt, it was now sealed with asphalt, roughly spread all the way down to the cove. Unlike her younger years, she could now traverse the path without slipping.

She sat on a rock and watched the ebb and flow of the Derwent River. Some children, accompanied by their parents, were playing in the sand, filling up their buckets, inspecting the marine life in the water left behind at low tide. *Children will always love this place,* she thought. She could hear their laughter above the noise of the waves. None here would be aware of what had happened on the black rocks a long time ago and that was as it should be. She sat for a long-time reminiscing. For the most part, it was a happy time for her and the affection she had for her grandparents and Aunt Pat still rested deep inside her.

She reluctantly left her peaceful, treasured place and went to visit her second cousin, Hector, and his wife. She adored them. When the time came it was a poignant moment, saying goodbye.

Then she visited her grandparent's grave where her mother was also buried. Seeing Kathleen and Harold Whitman's names still brought her to tears. Lastly, she sat near her adored Aunt Pat's grave and lamented how heartbreaking it was. Her beautiful aunt was long dead before she began living the happy life she hoped for with that bastard Cecil. Flowers were gently laid on the graves and words to her loved ones were softly spoken. Rebecca looked up at the sky knowing it was a bit silly, but she hoped they could hear her. Rebecca caught her plane home.

'Are you all right?' Andrew asked as she rushed towards him on arrival at the airport lounge. He placed his arm around her waist while walking towards the baggage pick up area.

'Eric and his wife were very gracious. They were glad I'd come to see them. I think that might be the last time I go back to Hobart. I don't have the need to see it anymore. I'll tell you all the details over a cup of tea when we get home. So glad to be back. I'm at my happiest when I'm with you, Andrew.'

He held her closer as they waited by the bag carousel.

About the Author

Elizabeth Long was born and grew up in Hobart, Tasmania. In her late teens she moved to Melbourne, mainly to explore the experience of a bigger city. She liked it so much she stayed.

Over the years her working life involved administrative roles, and while satisfying, her true love has been anything to do with the arts.

She performed in many plays for a local amateur theatre company and also makes large mosaic art works, as well as writing one-act plays.

These interests have resulted in winning awards. She loves art galleries, film, museums, domestic animals, wildlife and reading. Writing, however, is what she liked to do most of all. It was considered her best subject at school.

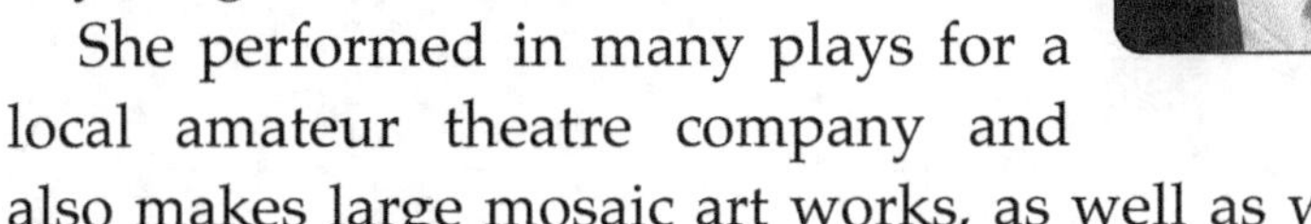

Her first published novel is *The Taroona Incident*. *A Body in the Lane*, a spinoff, is her latest book. She is excited to bring this to you, the reader.

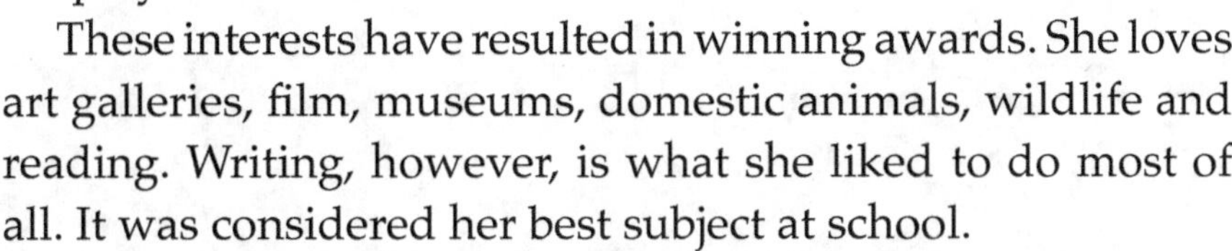

Elizabeth likes to explore the human condition, how people cope with tragedy, and why some commit a crime. Her favourite genre is mystery/drama fiction or crime fiction.

Acknowledgements

Coroners Court, court admin – for information about what happens to a body that is not identified.

Detective Senior Constable Brianna Gibson – for assisting me with police procedures. Her knowledge was invaluable.

Anna Bilbrough, editor – for her expertise, assistance, helpful ideas and diligence in bringing my novel to readiness.

Busybird Publishing – who are always encouraging, caring and provide a helping hand throughout the publishing process. Without them my book would never emerge.

Maggie Turner – for her outstanding layout and typesetting. Her attention to detail and design has resulted in an easier, relaxing, read and beautiful presentation.

My husband – whose scrutiny always finds my typos.

My family and friends – for their ongoing support.

The Taroona Incident

Elizabeth Long

A body.
A secret.
A reckoning.

When four-year-old Rebecca finds the lifeless body of her much-loved Aunt Pat in the Derwent River in 1952, the course of her life changes forever. Plunged into loss, despair and grief, Rebecca navigates the years that pass like a boat searching for shore.

Cecil Newton hides in many ways. Running from a past he doesn't want to face, he moves from town to town, burying his secrets and hoping they stay hidden.

When years pass and paths cross, the past comes ashore. Rebecca meets the truth. Cecil meets fate.

The Taroona Incident is a mystery that spans generations and delves into the question of who we are, and explores who we need to become if we're to survive.

busybird
publishing

Busybird Publishing is a boutique micropublisher based in the heart of Montmorency, Victoria.

We publish a handful of titles yearly, trying to combine quality and entertainment with some altruistic outcome, e.g. raising awareness for a particular condition (as our glorious coffee table photography book, *Walk With Me* – a journal of Kev Howlett's trek up to Mount Everest Base Camp and back – raised awareness of Charcot-Marie-Tooth disease), and/or donated a portion of proceezds for books to various foundations (such as Women Helping Women, Breast Cancer Victoria, the Prostate Cancer Foundation, the Epilepsy Foundation, Vision Australia, and, with this book, to the Indigenous Literacy Foundation).

We also run workshops on various forms of writing (fiction, nonfiction, memoir), publishing, and photography, and an annual two-day writing retreat; host a monthly Open Mic Night (the third Wednesday of every month); and hold competitions to help aspiring writers get published or win mentoring.

To learn more about Busybird Publishing, check out our website at **www.busybird.com.au**.